South

CHIP MARTIN grew up in California and has lived in London since the early 1970s. He writes criticism under the name Stoddard Martin. His novellas, published by Starhaven, include the sequences *A School of London* and *The End of the Road*.

WILLIAM WILKINS' 'San Giorgio Maggiore and the Zitelle, Venice' provides the cover image for this book. He is represented by the Martin Tinney Gallery, Cardiff. <www.artwales.com>

GW00601052

SOUTH

two novellas

Chip Martin

ISBN 0-936315-24-5

STARHAVEN, 42 Frognal, London NW3 6AG
in U.S., c/o Box 2573, La Jolla, CA 92038
books@starhaven.org.uk
www.starhaven.org.uk

Typeset in Dante by John Mallinson
Printed by CPI, 38 Ballard's Lane, London N3 2BJ

Contents:

IN THE WIND

The three great stimulants of decadents: innocence,
artificiality, and brutality...

– Nietzsche

1.

It was Seward Barnes who introduced us to Lydia. He had been
talking about her since the previous fall when we'd gone with
him to a Vintage Rolls-Royce Owners' meeting. Seward was a
rich kid Tony had known in college. He was as galumphing, loud
and uncouth as Tony was lean and earnest. I would never have
had anything to do with him if it hadn't been for Tony. Why
Tony hung out with him I wasn't sure. Later I realized that he
wasn't as 'not into' people like that as he pretended.

Seward was a hedonist, Tony a rebel – at least that's how
they were playing it back then. I was a silly love-struck post-teen
wearing billowy dresses of old crêpe and knee-high boots that
made me too tall as well as too big, especially with my ruff of
Goldrush hair. Seward would've been a better match for me,
physically. Lydia might've been perfect for Tony. But I'm getting
ahead of my tale.

We spent the day in a vineyard near Sunnyvale. Rich, would-
be rich and middle-aged stylers – all the owners of Rollses and
Bentleys were there, to show off their Flying Ladies. It seemed

pretty tacky to me, being a child of the Renaissance Art Fair, all those men in jumpsuits and women fanning themselves with pink kleenex. Necklines of sixty-year-olds plunged between what could be pushed up in bras from Frederick's of Hollywood – it was that end of the Bay Area.

I lolled on a swing in the shade of a live oak while Tony neglected to look at me. A hot wind lifted my skirt like an awning, but no one seemed to care what colour underwear I wasn't wearing. Seward had brought some wine his Granddaddy had 'liberated' after the War. Nobody believed in that story, but then no one seemed to notice the fungus on the corks either, which is why I got sick.

We drove home along Skyline under the stars. I was curled up in back trying to find calm while they sat up front, Seward being macho.

''mazing the way these babies corner, huh?'

He shouldn't have bothered. Tony was off in some fantasy of mid-peninsula lights. He hated cars anyway.

'Can't we stop?' I moaned.

'Damn hot wind's gonna ruin 'er, though. Keep yer eye on that gauge.'

Reluctantly Tony moved his eyes to the dashboard.

'When it gets to a hundred…'

'Nine'y-seven, it says.'

'Can't we stop please?'

'Nine'y-eight… Ninety-nine…'

I was in trouble. Seward was reckless, but even he wasn't ready to blow up his Lady. So as steam started to billow through the floorboards, he veered off and I jumped out and ran halfway down a ravine to heave my guts.

Later, while he used a silk sleeve to play with the radiator cap and Tony sat on the running-board gazing at star-spangled night, I found myself walking along the ridge-top trying to get him to see me, I guess, as some cinematic myth-woman.

'Shit… gotta get a new cooling-system… do it in England.'

Tony peeled his eyes off. 'You're going to England?'

'Sure, man. June a few days, then South a France.'

'You know we were going?' – This made me cough; or maybe it was Seward's Acapulco Gold that he'd just passed a joint of.

'Going to Europe'? 'We'? – He'd made some pillow-talk about it when we first met, but I'd assumed it was just to get laid – not that he'd needed help to do that. To hear him say it now to a third-party – well, it just made my vagabond soul leap after a vision of the two of us dancing up the Spanish Steps.

'Far out,' Seward muttered. 'Did it two years ago.'

'What?'

'Bought the Rolls; trucked around England an' Europe – a gas.'

'But we're not going to travel,' Tony said. 'We're going to live in London.'

The wind seemed to calm down to listen.

'Why would ya wanna do that?' Seward asked.

'Tony's a songwriter now,' I piped up, as if that answered it.

He shot a look at me. 'Might write a riff or two.'

Seward smirked. 'So *that*'s why you're going to England?'

'Maybe other things too.'

'Hey don't get uptight, man. Be a songwriter if you want; less competition for the rest of us who wanna make a mill. But London's old, man, and a drag if you're not in with the right people; South a France's diff'rent. What we gotta do is get another limo an' go south; 'd be crazy… There's a chick I know who might go with us.'

'What "chick" is that, man?' – Tony sounded derisive: Seward was well-known as a klutz with the ladies.

Now it was his turn to be sheepish. 'She's just a friend. You'll dig her: gets loaded an' loons. A real fox, man. Got red hair – not like Lauren's; nothing's like that. But you'll see. She's a Leo.'

So that's how we first came to hear about Lydia. And I liked Seward better after he'd complimented me. But she hardly registered on me then, and definitely not as a rival. For some stoned reason, the way he described her made me think of my dog, who we'd left in our Beetle back in his drive – 'No way I'm gonna let that hippy mutt drool on my Phantom all day!' So I erupted:

'Omigod, the dog! Can't we go now please?'

Tony was stuck to the running-board. 'She's as obsessed with that pooch as you are with your Flying L, man.'

Maybe he was just trying to make Seward feel better. Still it pissed me off, so I kicked him before getting back in.

Seward turned to check the gauge – 'Too hot still' – but the ignition caught, and in a minute we were off again, careening back onto Skyline, veering like sea-sickness around those wide curves, leaving the stillness and lights of Bay far behind. Gears wound, horses heaved, hoofs pounded below us. Seward lashed his lady, me egging him on. Wind rushed through Tony's hair, scattering thoughts of my mutt, this other woman and some mythical Europa. Then the hissing began.

Steam seeped through the floorboards and, before we could pull over, billows were choking up. The world inside went invisible, clangs banged, metal scraped. Meanwhile, over it all Seward's voice surrealistically brayed,

'Far out, man. I'll give you her number. Call 'er when you get there – you'll dig her – she's a gas!'

So that's how, eight months later, we came to be paying homage to her in her chartreuse box of a flat above a shop in Parkway, Camden Town.

It was spring in England. After weeks of poetic shivering in what they called a 'bed-sit', we were lonely and ready for company – even foolish enough to imagine Seward's South of France lark as an option. His invitation, in fact, had been our passport for being let into her court.

She received us in a Chinese robe and made us sit listening to her holding forth on the phone like a little Napoleona. Her fluty words were haloed in puffs from a 'fag' and punctuated by vulgar slurps from a mug of Nescafé:

'I'm sorry,' she said to a receiver, 'I simply cannot understand why you birds want to live in such pain. If things aren't right with your bloke, you must go off on your own... Yes, but *love*, as you call it, is love, and a job is a job; and if you can't see this geezer as I've arranged, then I'm afraid you're off the agency altogether.' – She turned to us and stage-whispered, 'Thought I'd got rid of these indecisive trendies.' Then to the phone: 'Look, Rose, ring back when you've got it together.' She hung up. 'Where was I?'

She'd begun by giving us a compleat history of her life, assuming without question that we'd be interested.

'Chelsea,' my man obliged.

'Ah yes. I lived there seven years, you know – halfway between the Kings and the Fulham Roads. People dropping by on their way back and forth, half I'd never seen before, never would again… But up here on my own, well – things are going to be very much more – '

One phone rang – this being the days before separate lines, she had two. 'Lydia… Yes, I know exactly whot you're on about, Dion. When a relationship's got to the stage ours has got to – '

We were perched under windows on what she called a sofa – in fact, a shelf built in and covered with Turkish throws. An adjacent shelf covered with a mattress served as a bed, which was where she sat, enthroned. No other furniture cluttered the space, only records, magazines, books on astral projection and so on, a watchful pair of cats, an oversized TV and the phones, the second of which now rang.

'Hang about,' to the first. To the second: 'Lydia… Yes, well, I'm glad to hear that you've sorted it out, Rose.' To the first: 'I think it ought to be cooled a bit, Dion.' To the second: 'I'm behind you completely: he is a dreadful mistake.' To the first: 'Split up, did you say? Well, you don't have to be so eager.' To the second: 'You have this other bloke's address then, do you?' To the first: 'I expect you to continue coming round, Dion.' To the second: 'And do get the money *before* this time, Rose.' She hung up the second. To the first: 'Right then, bye.' – Hung up the first with a clack, then turned back to us:

'Such dramas! Where was I?'

Seward had called her a fox, and she was that. Hair straight and shiny, as if brush-red; lashes jet-black; eyes bead-like and heavy with make-up... She had a sharp nose and long teeth, browned at the edges from smoking. Overall, she struck you as too small for her nature, like a fox seems too small for killing.

'Business?' Tony asked, being politeness itself.

'Just dramas.'

She leaned forward for an ashtray, which let her robe fall open, exposing that part which had sent Seward into such abject lust – a breast abnormally large for her petiteness.

'What does your agency do, Lydia?' I asked puritanically, Tony's eyes having conspicuously widened.

'Hard to describe really...' She tightened the sash as if to pretend that our peep had been pure accident. 'I help out in various ways, you see. London's full up with wandering sparks – you must have sussed that by now.'

Her cheekbones were arched, her skin pinked by a network of veins. Her lips looked full because of the red lip-gloss; her body seemed slim, boyish, except for what she'd let us glimpse. Already I was aware that she'd try to get my man if I let her: try to fox him as surely as she had Seward with her saucy bark of a laugh and carious flow of words.

'Coffee?'

'Naw, I don't think.'

'Cup of tea then?'

'No thanks, I – '

She made him sound tongue-tied, as if she were his mother. 'Sure? Fancy something stronger?'

'I'll have another,' I put in.

Tony followed my lead. 'OK. Me too.'

'You do want it, don't you? because if you don't...' She made him sound completely ball-less, which, when it came to her, maybe he was.

'It's just that your English coffee and tea seem so strong,' he answered sensibly, making it worse.

'So strong?! I always thought you lot thought ours was too weak!' – With that, she sashayed out to her kitchen, wobbling on oversized platform heels and giggling as if someone had just told her the wickedest joke in the world.

We tried to agree that she was too tacky to think of and that Seward's plan had been Seward's folly. But no lady's bedchamber in California had ever interested Tony like that; and since London was as grim as Seward had predicted, dark and poor, he decided we ought to try the Lake District.

I didn't leave him a second to change his mind. Lending him half of my money to buy an ancient Volkswagen, I got us to drive north the very next day.

'It's so beautiful!' I marvelled as hour after hour we curved through emerald-jade hills, mottled by shadows of cloud.

'You hear that tapping?'

'What tapping?'

'That tap, in the engine.'

Lancashire. Westmoreland. Silence. More tapping.

After a few days, I ventured: 'What're you thinking about?'

'What does that mean?'

'I don't know,' I said, though after a while I added, 'I guess I was just wondering if you wanted to make love to Lydia.'

That made him pay attention to something other than his tapping.

'I'd mind a little,' I went on, as if only speculating. 'I know I shouldn't. I wouldn't so much if I felt we could share it…'

Hippie morality! You'd never catch me saying that now.

'Of course you'd mind,' he protested as the sky fell in red streaks. 'And I wouldn't, and don't think she would either. And I doubt that either of us'd tell you if we did.'

Tap, tap.

Windermere. The sun lying on me. I could feel it lighting my features and brightening my skin magically. Knowing I looked pretty, I spoke to him softly. He leaned up on an elbow and gazed out through the hills:

'Exhaling
'West Wind

'Driving spirit…'

Rewrite Shelley was what he was going to do, he announced. OK, I thought, if that's what you're into, and sketched in a blank page of his notebook while great, proud ideas led him up to the top of Hellvellyn. Visions, memories, scraps of old babble came to mind as I waited for some lyrical thought to bring him back down to me. Lord what fools we mortals, you might say…

Tap, tap.

'That goddamned Volkswagen puts me so uptight. Bloodless, mechanical…'

'Have another beer.'

We drank pissy bitter in dank northern pubs. That was our dinner and entertainment. No more Indian food like in London, not even a grudging good mood – we couldn't afford it.

If we couldn't afford it, then why had we trudged off to this sodden end of the world? So I wondered, but instead reminisced about California, trying to lighten it up:

'See that girl bare-footin' along
'Whistlin' and a-singin' she's a carryin' on…'

He just stared at me as if I was some zitty fourteen-year-old from the Valley trying to be a surfer girl.

'This trip might've been a mistake,' he finally muttered.

Amen. 'You think maybe we better go home?'

Did a glimmer of Lydia light up his cloud then?

On some mad intuition, I added: 'Or should we try Seward's South of France thing after all?'

Isn't it amazing, as she might've observed, what a silly bird is willing to do to hold onto her man?

*

Heat settled like a lid over London. Cars, bikes, busses, lorries all choked the roads south. Start, stop, clutch, brake… Bermondsey,

New Cross – we passed a dozen grim suburbs no one would ever have found on Ye Olde tourist maps. Unending congestion, unending fumes, cigarettes butt-to-butt – 'bloody awful'. It seemed as if their whole island race was migrating south on that L.A.-hot Sunday in June.

Talk was peppered with cracks about our Volkswagen. Seward hadn't bought a new Flying Lady since he'd blown his, so in his half-laughing, half-haughty way he was pretending it was our fault he had to travel in non-rich-kid fashion.

'All I had ta have was a decent co-pilot,' he brayed. 'All ya had to do was keep yer eye on that gauge...'

'You beat your own lady to death,' Tony stated.

'Whot are those two on about?' Lydia declaimed from in back, where she and I had been placed.

'Had ta buy a new engine 'cause this punk was drunk.' – Seward hung his head over his seat to ogle her. 'Spent all my money on it.'

'Not *all*, I hope.' – You had to chuckle at her blatancy. 'Do you understand them, Lauren?' she asked in a tone of 'aren't all men genetically inferior?'

'I was sick then,' I said.

Seward guffawed. 'Let's get loaded an' loon!'

He passed us a bomber, which may have been what provoked her to launch into one of those monologues that set the tone of the trip:

'O deah... O I do wish it weren't so far... But it's a good job we didn't take off sooner... had to endure such a drama between Rose and her bloke.'

''s he the cat where I scored the coke?'

'Is she the chick that's taking care of your cats?'

They were far too interested in her. Knowing as much, she rabbitted on, pretending it was just for my ears:

'I must tell you, Lauren; you'll find it fascinating. You see, Rose has been doing this scene with this geezer for some time now – years perhaps; I cahn't recall the details. At first she quite fancied him, but then, after a time, do you know, he began showing signs of being – well, rather uncool if you know what I mean. Whot was it he did? a musician, I think; something like that. But after a time do you know, he entirely stopped speaking? Can you imagine how boring and awful? O I've known musicians and that sort who sort of hold it all in their heads; but after a time do you know, I sussed that he didn't even make music really! Can you imagine? So finally I decided, well: if he can't even speak, then what is the point?'

'Let's smoke a joint!'

'So I told her.'

'Told her what?' Tony asked, weirdly entranced by this drek.

'To get it together to tell him to split, obviously. – O she was in such a state! Finally, I just had to insist that she come round to my place until... but she hadn't been in the door more than five minutes before he shows up all angry and 'orrible and dressed in those swastikas and ripped jeans, and right there in my front room where she was standing stroking the new kitten all lovely and frail, grabs her like this' – she latched onto my wrist – 'and demands that she go with him. Well: even before his ugly great mitt had hurtled down on her face, I was up and battering and demanding he get out before I called Old Bill! But... O I do hate violence of whatever sort, don't you?'

Seward leaned on the horn. 'Let's get movin'!' he hooted.

The traffic into Ramsgate was like smog over San José. 'So what happened?' Tony asked, shoving his hand off.

'What happened to whom?' – Her tone suggested the question was hopelessly daft.

'Did she go with him or stay with you?'

'But don't you see? that hardly makes any difference. The point is simply –'

'That we're on the road!' hoorayed Seward. 'Come on, Lyddie: let's get loaded an' looooooon!'

We made the hovercraft just in time for our booking and crept in that eerie, amphibious bird across the Manche and salt-flats.

On we sped through Calais with not a blink from the Customs ('Stick the coke in yer pants, Laure – come on, be a sport!') Whirring gears into high, late, Gitane-scented sunset, we saw Mercedeses whiz by, Citroëns, Maseratis…

'I gather it's not "hip", as you and Tony might define it; but it *would* be a joy to be in one of those rockety things just now.'

'Shoulda just shot ourselves through the timewarrppp!'

Grumpy from driving, Tony observed: 'How can someone as factual as you believe in that sci fi crap, Seward?'

'It's as factual as anything else, Tone.'

'If it's so factual then give me some proof.'

'Look man, when Einstein first said Relativity's *it*, no one believed him. He didn't have to have proof, man. But extend Einstein's theory, break the speed a Light, an' the whole concept of Time'll break down!'

Rolling green, velvet skies, sycamore avenues… star-bright universe lit by crescent moon, yellow headlamps…

'I know whot Seward's on about,' Lydia weighed in.

'OK, so don't believe it, Tone. But then everything else Einstein predicted turned out to be true, so – '

'I can accept breaking the speed of light. But the concept of Time – '

'That's exactly what breaking the speed a light means! Look, if you shoot a ball-bearing down a line at the speed of light – '

On as if hell-bent, stop only for peeing. Methadrine tablets, astrological chat… O what vasty visions in that tender night!

'Why is it you cahn't just believe?' she challenged.

'I can believe,' Tony said. 'But not if someone just tells me some theory that's never been proved. I mean, it's just myth until there's some logical – '

'That's exactly what I been saying if you'd only listen' – Seward.

'And it's a great myth: it has purpose: it inspires people to think the impossible. But – '

'"Purpose"?' she hooted.

Voices rising and falling, as if backing some rock-band; then a glowing sun rising, sidewalk in Dijon, café au lait…

'Because if what Einstein said is true and that ball-bearing is going the speed a light, then everything in the universe'll be focused in on it.'

'Yeah, man. Some basic purpose for the three an' a half billion people on this planet, not some airy delusion.'

'Personally, I can believe all these things,' she mused. 'They're just things I seem to know intuitively. I don't need your proofs or your facts. I just know when they are true. I have faith.'

Heat. Funk. Sun too bright for night-trippers… Lyons for lunchtime: vanishing appetite… Avignon, start, stop; no more talk; smells of olive oil, evergreen… Then at last, autoroute above the Côte d'Azur…

A mild westerly blew as we came into St Tropez. It sped Lydia and Seward into a café, leaving Tony and me to marvel at a scene like Newport Beach superimposed on *Zorba the Greek*. But someone had to find a place to stay before we could sit around gawking; and my man was all responsibility that day, even after doing the driving. He located a landlady who led us out of town, rattling up a dirt road.

At one turn, an ancient farmer glared at us as if he'd just as soon shoot the next tourist who tripped onto his turf; then we were deep into fig bushes and oleander and pulling up next to a 'villa' where, as sun set, we settled in plastic armchairs on a patio looking west at the Golfe and lights of Ste Maxime beyond. This would be home now, no more mindless motion. Almost on the instant I was dreaming of Marin.

The landlady meanwhile practised her Franglais on Tony, trying to sell us on another villa further up in the hills, just a little 'plus cher'. But my man was thrifty, so her commerce trip failed. Thus we were left in peace to make love in a heart-stopping twilight, before Life in the Fast Lane revved into action again.

2.

When I think back on it now, it's easy enough to see how vacuous we were at that stage – bored stiff, though we didn't know it; spoiled rotten, though we never admitted it to ourselves. We thought we were having fun then, but what is *fun* anyway? In the decades since, I've had fun many times, or thought so. But that doesn't help me define what it meant to us then.

There were sounds. There were colours. There were feelings and hopes you had, because you were young. But these things flew past: you recalled mostly the pain – the swelling discontent of being close enough to touch something you longed for but just couldn't reach, or just could for a moment before it blew away...

We had arrived then. The season hardly begun, restaurants on the quai were half-full and eager. Designer trendies and groups of bourgeois northerners strolled along the promenade gawking... 'Who's yaucht is thaut, Nigel?'

'I say, Samantha, I believe thaut one must be the Duke of Westminister's.'

'Duke of Westminster. Do you know him, dahling?'

'I was on it once. In Doughville, I believe.'

'En Deauville? Oh really? How elegant.'

'Yes. They needed a fourth.'

'A fourth?'

'Sure. They had all the fifths they needed, haha!'

Seward was the one most determined to have fun, even if no one laughed at his jokes. Interspersed with guffaws, he stared at rich kid toys in the harbour. He had a hunger for them that made you almost sympathize with him.

Lydia's passion, by contrast, wasn't for things. 'O whot shall we do without people?' she whined.

'People?'

'Yes, other people.'

'You mean frogs?'

'I mean pee-pull!'

'I know some crazies in Monte,' Seward announced. 'Maybe we can go up there one day.'

The idea seemed to daunt him. He gnawed on a nail.

'This coke is ruining my appetite,' she meanwhile sniffed.

'Salade de crudités? 'sieur? Oeuf dur mayonnaise, 'dame?'

Boredom threatened. Again, a sniff-sniff.

'Tonight's our anniversary,' I offered.

'Coquille St Jacques? 'dame?'

'Anniversary?!' she scoffed.

'Calamares à l'Armoricaine?'

'It's been a year to the day since Tony and I met.'

Engrossed in his egg, my man seemed not to hear.

A girl in loose whites and chestnut hair passed playing 'L'Arlésienne' on a flute.

'Where'd you two meet anyways?' Seward asked over a mouthful of squid.

'It was at – '

'O yeah, I remember. That wedding. Divorced now.'

'Divorced?!' – Lydia's tone made him choke.

'They're back together again, Seward,' I corrected.

'Nope.' – He was adamant. 'Split up, for good.'

The flute solo continued. It was ache-makingly tender.

Tony asked, 'You seen 'em, Seward?'

'Sure. In the Co-op Market. He was chasing her around with a broken bottle. Haha.'

'In the Common Market?!' Lydia trilled.

'Vegetable section!' he exploded. – He was such an ass! 'Hahaha.'

The flute girl passed on. We finished our starters. The waiter reappeared:

'Coq au vin? 'sieur? Brochette d'agneau? Poulet rôti?'

'Ooo my strides are too tight' – Lydia.

'I thought you couldn't eat' – Seward.

'And I could've had the same pair for five quid in Chelsea.'

'And I pay nine so you can have something that says Saint Trop on it!'

'Don't be dahft. It's just so hard to get things to fit me properly...' She thrust out her bust as if to adjust a strap, and we all had to take note: *that* of course made everything different.

Mercifully, just before Tony froze into a permanent gape, she was upstaged by two French boys, very tanned and dressed in loose white as well. One of them was playing Peruvian pipes and a drum while the other passed through the tables offering roses in varying shades of red and pink.

'How beautiful!' I mused.

Tony's eyes dropped to his coq.

'I want a mauve one!' Lydia announced.

'To match your kleenexes?' Seward happily smirked.

The waiter reappeared to shoo the boys away just as they were getting to us. Caught in that enchanting, primitive sound, I watched them pass, until they were eclipsed by an Australian folk-rocker yodelling a verse of 'Dead Flowers'.

'Fromage ou dessert, 'sieurs, 'dames?'

'Kel ayspess doo daysert avay voo?'

'Shouldn't we have given them something?' I asked, spellbound.

'Ooo I fancy that great strawberry thing with whipped cream!'

'What about your strides?'

'How do you say it?'

'Fraise melba,' Tony mumbled, clearing his mouth.

'Frez melbah seel voo play...'

> 'When yer sittin' back
> 'In yer gold-pink Cadillac,
> 'Takin' bets on Kentucky Derby day –'

'Bahbahbumpa,' Seward mimicked.

'Am I being too extravagant?' – her.

'Sure!'

'Ooo good!'

> 'I'll be in my basement room
> 'With a needle, and a spoon;
> 'Another girl will take my blues away – '

On the decks of the yachts, *they* took coffee. On the benches of the quai, hippies sat with backs ostentatiously turned. In the foreground the Australian yodelled while, to one side, an Algerian music-critic was busy trying to kick-start his motopied – 'Rumbra-rumbra-rumbra-braummmm...'

'Ringadingadingadinga!' Seward mimicked, delighted.

'The one thing I don't like about marriage,' Lydia said via a mouthful of cream, 'is that bit about "Death us do part".'

'Marriage is nowhere,' Tony remarked, clearing his plate.

I glared at him.

'Ringadingadingadinga!' Seward spluttered.

'I used to think that,' Lydia observed, 'in a cynical part of my life I'm glad to be done with...'

> 'Take me down, little Susie, take me down;
> 'I know you think you're the queen of the Underground – '

'The vows I liked best,' I said, 'were at a wedding in Portola Valley. They were married by a friend who'd become a minister in the Universal Life Church. He said: "Nothing I say will change what has already happened for them; all we here are doing is giving affection and support for what they've already done in their hearts".'

'That is lovely!' – She engorged a last mouthful.

'You can buy a ministry in the Universal Life Church for twenty-five dollars,' Tony stated.

'Ringadingadingadingapffff.'

Lydia stared at him as if she couldn't believe what she'd heard. 'He's right,' I admitted.

'But of course, it makes no difference whatsoever,' she chastised. 'Marriage is a spiritual trip; it makes no difference who's saying the words or why he is saying them, or what words he's chosen to say – don't you see? Apparently that's exactly what Lauren's geezer was on about, Tony. You missed the point entirely, as you so often do.'

'I try not to listen to bullshit,' he muttered.

'Apparently you also don't listen to words! and your wanting to be a poet or songwriter, or some such... Words can be very, very beautiful, you know. Or perhaps you don't, though one would've thought that you should.'

'So some Jesus-freak says it! it's still just a myth. No hip marriage is going to be any different from – '

I got up then. He'd hit where it hurt, and he knew it.

Of course, on any rational basis I had to agree with him: marriage was nowhere in my hip book either. But to say so so bluntly in front of a person like her could only look like rejection, which was exactly the picture she was longing to paint.

'Yup, he was beatin' her over the cabbage in the Common Market, haha!'

'I am sorry, Tony,' I heard her voice going as I flounced off. 'I know at least one marriage that is different – they live in Portobello, and they are quite different. And I assure you their marriage is quite another thing!'

'Lauren?' he called out.

'You mean Rose an' her uptight boyfriend? They live in Portobello, don't they? Ringadingadadinga, wheeeeee!'

On the way to the car, she walked arm-in-arm with Seward. All the way home in the back, they giggled and guffawed. I wanted to hold Tony's hand and make up with him, but that was the last thing she was after. When we got to the villa and went off to our separate rooms, her performing became more insistent. A thin wall couldn't protect us as we undressed; by the time we were in between the sheets, a yelp had come from her, then one of Seward's guffaws. Finally, the head of one of their beds started banging against the plaster as if suddenly, and counter to all her stipulations, they were going at it with a vengeance.

What was being jostled into Tony's mind then? Did he realize this act was for his benefit? Putting his lips on my neck, he brought me down on our own jammed-together little beds. Out the door wild dogs bayed while echoes of songs from the promenade faded behind stage-whispers out of their room. If only we could've lain there thoughtless letting the kissing and loving span the great nada of night, as we had in our best moments before! But again her smutty laughing intruded, and Tony's kisses got wetter and more indefinite until, in the end, it was just me making love to him, and it was over way too quickly.

I lay there awake. He fell asleep; she'd gone silent. At last it was only Seward's snoring that bored through the walls. Out on the patio a warm breeze rose and fell, carrying sounds of the night. Distant cars, katydids, crackling undergrowth... I remembered the dogs that had roved toward the house in the day, only to run off through thickets when they caught sight of us. I could hear them as they moaned now but not see them. On the edge of the mattress I lay thinking: it was so wild here, so different from what we'd known in our leafy American 'burb...

In the morning, I slept while the others got up and went into town to get coffee – one of the imperial rituals of *her* régime. In bed I half-drifted, until the protestant work-ethic, or something, made me shake a leg.

Still in my nightie, I went out on the patio with a pair of Tony's Levi's she'd lampooned – 'That awful droopy bum! I must teach you Americans some style...' I was going to mend them, but after a time I heard nails patting the flagstones behind me and turned to see reddish hair and a long face gazing up.

'O it's all right, viens ici. Viens, chien. Bon chien. Chienne?'

Paps swung low under her belly. Ducking her head warily, she sniffed her way toward me. Then on some dumb instinct, she was into my shadow and letting me reach out to her.

'O girl, it's all right. Viens ici. Viens, chienne.'

Her coat was matted; from one of her eyes, fluid oozed. A swollen tick was stuck to her chest like a medal; I tried to pick it out, but she jerked away. On her neck were crusted scabs; as soon as I touched one, she backed off.

'Sucre, chienne?' – I offered a lump of the sugar Lydia used for her Nescafé. 'Viens. Ici, chienne, ici.'

Kneeling, I tried to coax her to eat.

In the meantime, unbeknownst to me, a man had come out on the patio from the last room in the villa, the one on the far side of Seward and Lydia's. I have no idea how long he'd been there before his voice said,

'Elle est timide.'

The oleanders seemed to quiver.

A smooth, dark-haired figure in red swimming briefs, he stood against green, pine-ridged hills, bisecting and partly hiding the tile roof of another villa further up there.

'Trop de gens l'ont battue,' he explained.

His smile was a killer. He was possibly the most classically good-looking man I'd ever seen.

'Elle est venue avant que – ?'

'Si, si. Elle a faim. Il y a beaucoup comme ça.'

The sky was cloudless, blue, fading into heat-haze. I looked at it to keep from staring, while my guest slurped the last of the sugar from my hand.

'Non plus, chienne.'

'Il n'y en a plus? Moment...' He ducked in his double-doors and came back out with a handful of biscuits, which he tossed into the drive at his end of the patio.

Pattering over, the dog gobbled them up.

'Il y a beaucoup comme ça?' – Feeling obliged to make small-talk, I dredged my memory of high school French.

'Si, si. The people bring them and abandon. Après, it is necessary that she wander. You have seen the wounds on her neck? She must fight the other dogs for the food. Perhaps she is beaten also. Perhaps she is looking for food near a house and the people come beat her.'

'O c'est mauvais!'

'Si, for the dogs. For the people also. Mais elle est libre, n'est-ce pas?' – He spread his palms out to indicate no more biscuits; shaking her jowls, the beast went on sniffing for crumbs.

The man turned his attention now fully on me.

'Mais, you speak very well le français. Peut-être après six mois en France you will speak perfectly?'

I pinkened. 'Nous ne restons pas ici si longtemps.'

'Non? Eh bien, c'est dommage.'

His stare was interrupted by the dog's woof. We looked to the drive and saw its stones spitting up under the wheels of the Volkswagen...

'Ooo I say!' – Lydia's voice was the first to penetrate.

'Go on, dirty bitch!' commanded Seward, crunching over – the oleanders rustled as she beat a retreat from a fistful of stone. 'Dog's got the mange, Lauren. Shouldn't let it near.'

I said nothing. The know-all plopped in a chair beside me.

'Well I've had my proper coffee,' Lydia announced following him, as if this was all you'd been wanting to know.

'Yeah, and we had to hear all about her bowel problems,' Tony grumped, bringing up the rear.

'It's a bloody sight more than you had to talk about' – she whisked her lean bum onto a seat he was about to sit in – 'except to complain about prices, as usual.'

Thus put down, he went inside.

Lydia gazed after him assessingly. Then she noticed me looking the other direction, at the Frenchman, who had now settled down to sunbathing just outside his door.

'Why don't these frogs decide?' Seward observed. 'Either wear real pants or no pants at all.'

'You mean bloomers, like you Americans? – Lauren, when you get through with Tony's, do you think you could have a go here?' She eyed Seward's surfing-jams with disdain. 'Or perhaps it's better just to let sleeping dogs lie.'

Tony reappeared in cutoffs and tennies.

'Gonna run, man?' Seward took up. 'Shouldn't run on the roads, ya know: hard on the legs, varicose veins.'

Tying his laces, my man didn't listen. In a moment, the slip-slap of his rubber soles was rattling down the drive.

Lydia gazed after him, then noticed me catching her look: 'O I do rather fancy that, don't you?' – Was she going to declare an interest outright? 'No not Tony' – she cocked an eye toward the Frenchman. 'This other, I mean.'

Was she was fishing? making an accusation?

'Queer as a three-dollar bill,' Seward said.

'Bent as a nine-bob note, is the expression... A good bum's essential, Lauren, don't you agree?'

'Either way a frog fag,' Seward concluded.

But she had had enough of him for one morning.

'O must you imagine every geezer who's not eighteen stone is a poof? Honestly Seward, I'm beginning to think you have some sort of problem.'

That sent him off... leaving her to study my new friend, whose eyes stayed closed, as if he were too deep in reverie to catch the surge and ebb of her chat.

'Yes. Just right in that department, I should say...'

When I refused to be drawn by this, she changed tack:

'I think I fancy a bit of shopping this apray-meedee. You drive, don't you? Or no: Tony does all the driving, does he?'

If she thought she was going to get me to play cat with her, she was wrong. Determinedly virtuous, I kept my eyes on my needle and thread.

Seward meanwhile reappeared in a pair of shiny trunks and gold Adidas and departed in the direction Tony had vanished, only more galumphingly. Lydia gazed after him for a time, then noticed me not looking.

'I do admire relationships like yours,' she mused. 'I've been searching for years now; only recently have I decided not to bother. Something will turn up in the end, I know... I've had things in the past, see, but eventually, well – I came to understand that something just wasn't right... The first time it took two years before I sussed. – You and Tony have perfection, don't you?... because if there's one thing I've sussed it's that if something isn't right – if it doesn't feel all right – then you must break off and set out on your own. It might take months, or years even – I went six months in agony after I split with Dion. But then one morning, all of a sudden it was, I woke up to the fact that I'd done the right thing. What a daft little cow I'd been to wait!'

I could've ignored this. Instead, I decided to pretend to be as innocent as she imagined, or hoped, I was:

'But don't you have a sense, Lyddie, that it, like, takes time. That you have to, like, keep working even if it's – '

'Lauren, you must go by your feelings.' – She adopted the tone of a mother or snitty big sister. 'You can spend the rest of your life wondering. It simply must feel right, if it's to work – *all* right, I mean. If it isn't perfect, then you simply must split and go off on your own.'

That was her line. And I would hear more of it – much more, until I was fed up and things took a turn so that we wouldn't have to hear any of it ever again.

Why did I follow them that afternoon? It seems reckless to me now. He wasn't going to do anything with her, and I felt pretty sure that she couldn't get any further with him than laying some groundwork. But I was getting fried to a crisp – my Celtic skin couldn't take it like theirs: I was a real redhead, not a henna facsimile. So when Seward said he was bored with the beach and wanted to go into town to see if maybe he could talk his way onto one of the yachts, I got up to go with him. Then halfway to the car, I was sick of his yak and, not wanting to sit alone at the villa, I turned back to the beach. But by then, they had already set out.

I've never been sure whether Tony was semiconsciously trying to feel his way into a thing with her or if it was just a secluded beach he was after, good Northern Cal boy that he was. What she was up to wasn't in doubt: it was as transparent as fly-paper as you watched those piano-legs wobble on their ridiculous platforms behind his bare feet.

'A secluded beach?!' – She was using the tone she took when she wanted to make him seem like a dork; I followed without trying to hide or catch up. 'Honestly, where are you off to in such a flush?' – With that trim little butt of his leading her on, he could afford to be cool, little shit. 'Cahn't we stop for a coffee?'

If he'd wanted to ditch her, he could have then. Instead, he sat with her in the beach café she flounced into, among the rich and would-bes.

I went to the bar, keeping just out of sight, and drank citron pressé while she studied her make-up, adjusted her bikini and discoursed on the state of her tan. 'O deah, I do wish I could tell how my back is doing…'

'Un peu rosé.'

She laughed as if this were incredibly witty. 'O deah!'

After too much of that, he led her on further, up to the north end of Tahiti plage and off the sand onto the rocks. I held back now so as not to be seen; his moccasins, which I'd sewn for his birthday, and the balance of his legs made him seem like some Indian or old-style Arab guiding the grande dame across desert sands. At one point he turned but didn't spot me or, if he did, didn't let on. 'You're an urban northerner,' he meanwhile murmured to her as she teetered precariously over a scarp of razor-edged shale.

'If you mean by that that I'm out of breath, you're quite right… but I could be… quite fit if I wanted. I was… quite athletic once, when I was… younger. Did you suss? I was quite a good… runner in school. Runs in the… family. My father was… quite a good – Hello?'

Looking up, she discovered that he'd vanished. Scrambling down a boulder, I kept out of her eye. Did a sense of my presence unsettle her subconscious?

'All this ridiculous speeding about…' She scanned the horizon, hand over brow. 'Where's he gone, the dahft twit?'

Struggling around a stooped pine, she failed to notice my shadow above. The path stopped abruptly; she looked back, I ducked. That safe length of beach where bodies lounged in Bain de Soleil must have seemed a world away to her now.

'Tony?' she called out, as if in alarm; whereupon a faint cry wafted up from offshore, where he was doing the backstroke. 'Dahft twit,' she repeated under her breath and, wobbling, slipped down a dirt palisade to the cove where he'd relieved himself of his cutoffs.

After a moment of loitering, arms akimbo, looking every one of her years, she set to primping. Eventually finishing that, she lit a fag and perched on a rock like the little mermaid. Gazing as if with no interest to where he emerged from the soup, she'd fixed on just the right mask of carelessness by the time he'd arrived to present himself full-frontal.

'O!' she trilled as if scandalized. 'Good swim, was it?'

He shook the water out of an ear. 'Lovely,' in mock-British.

They were in a narrow space protected from breeze. It was stifling up in the pines where I'd hidden but even hotter down there, and the drops on his skin vanished quickly. Still breathing hard, he gazed back half-embarrassed at the blue-green he'd come out of. Knowing full well she was getting an eyeful, he let his chest rise and fall, muscles twitch and so on.

'Yes…' she drawled, regaining her cool. 'Rather impressive.'

'You can call me Apollo,' he tried.

'Really? A bit on the small side, don't you think?'

I might've laughed out loud if he hadn't been mine. 'Sour grapes,' he muttered, flopping down on his belly.

'Sour whot?!' – As if on cue, she reached her hands behind her, unhooked the bra-strap and let those big berthas loose.

'Cowgirl in the sand?' he murmured, trying to regain some advantage.

'Venus of the Rocks, I should think, if we keep to your gods.'

That was good – good enough that it was all either of them could manage for a while… Murmurs of sea and the late afternoon; then with perfect calculation, she began to oil her breasts.

'Do you do this sort of thing often?' she asked as if idly.

'What "sort of thing"?'

'This thing of going to secluded spots and putting on naked silence?'

He couldn't think of any clever response to that.

'Doesn't Lauren come with you?' – Bitch! 'Do you think I've put enough on?' – She kept coaxing him to look. 'I don't fancy burning, you know...'

'You'll live,' he muttered, dropping his head.

Having failed with that gambit, she lit a new fag.

'O deah,' she exhaled. 'O, but I do think it's lovely, all this lovely warmth and... quite a shame Lauren cahn't get into it. Reminds me of Corsica...'

'What?' he murmured; and that proved all she needed to launch into her big aria:

'O the sea and the sun and the late afternoon... When I was eighteen and just on my own, I went to Corsica, to make a film. It was quite the trendy thing for its time – nudity, free ideas and such; all the things I was into then, which is why we did it in Corsica, as well as the beauty... It was so beautiful. We were there several weeks – cahn't recall the facts precisely, but it hardly matters now. I met a young Corsican lad. He was very beautiful; dark, warm. Spoke no English and not much French really – some dialect, sort of Arabic or Italian perhaps. I spoke very little French at the time, so we communicated without words. We would lie about like this, naked, in silence – it was so beautiful. He would come to the beach in the dark after dinner when his family thought he was asleep. We'd make love and drink wine and make love; and then in the dawning he'd slip away... They were simple, his family, protecting; strong Catholics, I believe. O he was lovely... Tony, are you listening?... He'd come to me as if out of nowhere, in the dark... as if out of some heaven, but – he was so real! And very serious too, like you rather. Yes! I hadn't thought of it till now... I told him he was the first I'd ever had, which was very nearly true at the time; I was still only a silly teenager. He was in love with me. O, I was daft to leave...'

A breeze trembled the needles by my leg as she waited, expectant. His response, when it came, was flat as you get:

'Where was this?'

'O I cahn't tell the facts now – secluded spot, island or something; peninsula perhaps. Quite far from the cities, it was; facing south, I remember – yes, the wind was so warm... His family was the most important in the village. Lovely. He wanted to marry, but...'

She was sitting there with her chest thrust out to the waters, proud as a nymph on the prow of a skiff. But did he react? – Not in the slightest. Why? Had he seen me? Didn't he 'fancy' her, as she'd say? Or did she (and this was what I feared most) just bemuse and entrance him so much that he wasn't brave enough to poke her and get it over with?

'I wonder how Seward's getting on with his yachts?' she broke the silence to muse. – When you can't succeed with seduction, try gossip, eh?

'Shit!' he exclaimed.

'Bit over-the-top, isn't he?'

'You can't ever feel anything when you're rich.'

'O?' – She sensed leverage. 'How do you mean?'

'Only that, when you're into material things like he is, and money, you don't ever have time to really *feel*... I mean, he's all on the surface. Doesn't really stop to feel. I mean, sensually.'

'Ah,' she intoned, drawing the syllable into three. 'I see... Well, I suppose a person's born with feeling, as you put it, or he isn't. Isn't he?'

Tony sat up and stared at ripples over the shoals.

'I mean, either it's there or it isn't. Isn't it?'

The breeze was coming in more steadily now. Beyond their shelter, above the ripples, little white plumes were being drawn out toward deeper blues.

'Either it happens or it doesn't, doesn't it? Tony?... Well?'

There it was.

He peered around at her. She was all ready for him, nipples perked up, lips puckered, smile spreading to the limit her London pride would allow. Did it let him notice the brown at the edge of her teeth? Could he glimpse the predatory smallness and sharpness of them? Could he see how their setting would grow pinched in time, asymmetrical, and much sooner than mine would? – What made him turn then, pulling his knees to his chest? As he gazed again to the wavelets, shoulder to her, was it only male shyness that was getting at him?

She didn't think so. Clutching her top up and lighting a new fag, The Woman Scorned declaimed:

'Actually, I think you're quite wrong about the rich – and about Seward, if you'd like to know. I'm sure he's quite "sensual" in his own way.'

'Seward? Hey, I went all through school with the guy and – '

'I'm quite sure he could be quite good with a woman,' she concluded. 'If the right one were interested.'

That brought his ego down a peg.

To put a knife in, she added:

'And not just at keeping one on a lead!'

3.

When I was a pre-teen, I was a real puffball and never thought anyone I'd want would want to take up with me. Still, there was nothing I longed for more than to kiss and be kissed. I used to moon around listening to rock-n-roll love songs and dreaming of somebody indistinct. Was he dark, tall, silent and foreign, or burly and affectionate, like my Belgian Shepherd, who I would cuddle obscenely? God, I tripped on it! wrapping him up in huge hugs, eyes shut and lips moist, hair floating off wild like that poster of some princess drowning my older sister had pinned to her wall... She'd tease me without let-up. But then, at long last, he arrived – not tall and dark, or podgy and cheerful, but beautiful and sharp and full of no nonsense. Why did I go for it? Was it just desperation, like she said? I was no puffball anymore: I had the allure of a hip young New Woman by then. I could have had others, but I chose him – ran after him, loved him; God, how I did! my arms holding, my lips gobbling as if they could never get enough – all that *Seventeen* magazine shit. But now?

We lay in bed separate, each of us eavesdropping on the whispering through the flim-flam. We wondered, each for our particular reasons, what their cryptic chuckling was all about. Was Seward plotting to con his way onto some yacht and ditch us? Was Lydia truly making sloppy love to him, not just putting it on? Had she decided to become a realist and hook a rich kid while she had the chance? I didn't care, really. So far as I was concerned, the question was where our lives had come to if these creeps could be so important to us. Where was that 'purpose' Tony had been so idealistic about? Where were the 'real' things? the natural truths? the kind of certainties inside that meant maturity? Because that's what our generation had gone off looking for, wasn't it? meaning, authority, some value to base our lives on? Yet here we were still, mesmerized by conventions of 'fun'; still pursuing mirages as doggedly as any spoiled kids from any over-privileged time and place – Swinging '60s, Roaring '20s, you name it.

Self-contempt was our secret. It's why I got drunk. Seward, however, had no more coke for her to reign on. A dangerous turn lay ahead.

She would complain of no appetite at dinner. He'd order the most expensive thing on the menu to coax her to eat. Naturally Tony ordered us the cheapest: we were back on the can't-afford-a-good-time routine. This caused Seward to make a speech about looseness vs tightness and the good or bad life each could buy. Well, the good life carried on while hors d'oeuvres variés, langoustines in mayonnaise and côte de veau in white wine sauce were served – he gobbled it all up with obscene relish; Lydia picked; Tony ate sliced tomatoes and chips; I finished Lydia's chop. Then the bad one threatened over coffee, by which time even Seward had fallen silent.

St Trop for its part could not pull a long face. It was ready for its good life – the season was on now in earnest. Glasses tinkled; garçons moved like ballet-dancers balancing trays of apéritifs. Emerald menthe, yellow anis, vermouths pale and amber, pink pastis grenadine, crimson Camparis all were delivered and drunk. Meanwhile, in the harbour *their* yachts glittered with jewellery and chic; in the street garish cars and high-pitched motorbikes lurched; on the promenade all and sundry posed, gaped and moved on, circled and repassed to go do it all over again in front of somebody else.

'I shall not be forced into that bloody parade tonight!'— her.

'Shuddup, kid, an' drink!'

'O give it up, really! O, we do need people – look at the state we've come to.'

'Provence, isn't it?'

'Why doncha go up ta one a those yachts an' offer yourself?'

'Really, Lyddie: you're such fantastic entertainment.'

'Yeah, Lyddie: some "geezer" 'd love to kill time with you.'

'I think you lot are quite rude.'

'Aww. Stop teasing Lyddie.'

'Yes, quit teasing Lyddie,' she echoed, mocking tears.

'Ringadingadinga, haha!'

'That's it, Seward!' I put in. 'We could mime!'

'We could whot?'

'Pantomime.'

'Far out. You an' Terry roll up like two wheels; I'll stand in the middle kicking an' swearing; Lydia'll hunch over behind us, going "Rumbrumbrumzzhhh rumbrumbrumzzhhh". We'll be a plastic frog who can't start his motopied!'

'I've got a better one,' I enthused. 'We'll all go shoplifting!'

'Shoplifting?'

'Far out!' – He was game. 'Whacha do is steal everything out a one shop, take it down, put it in the next one, huh Lauren?'

'There's nothing cool about that,' Tony said, the kill-joy.

'All right,' I amended, 'we'll just do some straight miming. Go up to someone and mimic the stupid look on his face.'

I did this to him. Simultaneously, the Australian street-singer passed by banging 'Dead Flowers' again.

'Cool it,' Tony warned, 'or the waiter's going to – '

'Cool what?' I was no longer into doing a thing he said. 'Cool him?' – Standing, I began to ape the singer's gyrations.

'Yeah cool him, Lauren, ha!' – Only Seward of the four of us was as loose as me. 'Rumbabumbahbah Rumbabumbahbah – '

Suddenly a hand gripped my arm. 'Pas ici, Ma'moiselle, ce n'est pas gentil!' – It was the waiter.

'Hey, man!' I yanked myself free. 'What's he trying to do? Throw us out?'

The others had stood too. 'He's doin' it,' Seward smirked.

'Monsieur, je vous en prie – ' Tony began.

'Don't you apologize, Tony! He's nothing but a petty frog pig!' – Snatching Lydia by the arm, I crowed like a radical feminist: 'Come along, dear: let's you and I go find some peepull!'

Away we went, bouncing off bodies, hilariously in search of... God knows what I was up to that midsummer night!

Unlike me, she was sober as an abbess. When I think back on it now, I guess she was just waiting for the chance to break free – which came soon enough. Some dark little weasel tried to latch onto her, ogling the silver lamé thing that held up her tits. I knew she was 'not into that' even before she said it, so on some weird urge I lured him away. But by the time I'd dumped him and swirled back, she was nowhere to be found.

At first I felt jilted. Then I was starting to think how nice it might be to have the evening to myself when Seward and Tony kaleidoscoped into view.

They were loitering on the quayside looking at a grey, box-like construction moored between a pair of sleek, Newport Beach-style craft:

'It's not a yacht, Seward.'

'Sure it is, man. Crazeee!'

'That's a PT boat.'

'Now why would the U.S. Navy be in Saint Trop harbour, Tone? ain't exactly a military base. What you see there is one very far-out yacht.'

'Yeah. And your Uncle Jake's the captain.'

'Bet ya the next bottle, man.'

'How you going to find out?'

'Simple...'

Jamming his hands in his pockets, Seward ambled up to the gangplank, full of the resolve of a fourteen-carat lush. This left Tony to me, if I wanted. And I was just about to do something about it – i.e., our first sweet time together alone for a week, an idea of which was helping to shape me up and make me nicer by the second – when, like a bird of prey out of a nightmare, she swooped in.

'Toaneee?'

She threw out his name as if it were a spray of violets. He whipped around as if jerking out of a trance.

'O, so *here* you are...' She wobbled up to him on those absurd platforms, too self-absorbed to notice me. 'So where's our Seward then?' – *Our* Seward indeed!

He cocked a thumb at the yachts.

'Such a golddigger... Typical, isn't it?'

'Where's Lauren?' was all he said.

It was hardly the response she was angling for. Still, the cunning vixen kept at it:

'O you know the way she sort of raced off into the centre of things? ever so droll really; I was just along for the trip. She was doing exactly what she'd been saying: coming up behind people, mimicking their movements and... really you should've seen it. She's lovely, that chick.'

Her lilt brought to mind a beehived barmaid in the north of England who'd short-changed us while explaining to him how she'd loved Americans ever since the days when the GIs were 'overpaid, oversexed and over here'.

'Where is she now?' is all he came back with.

'Well, some geezer arrived – dark little frog – and started in. She was... O she was having a wonderful go at him, I think. To his pathetic delight, she took him by the arm and began imitating every word he said! Then I lost them in the crowd and came looking for... just wandering about till I happened on you.'

I could've doused her words with tabasco and crammed them down her throat. It wasn't *my* tits the 'little frog' had been ogling; and I'd only inveigled him off to help her!

Tony said nothing.

An American couple meanwhile strolled past with guitar and tambourine. They started in on 'Love the One You're With'.

'She'll be back any moment,' Lydia said, 'I should think.'

The message was 'You'll be lucky if she gets back tonight'.

She let it hover. After a time then, following his eyes to the singers, she observed:

'Any good this lot? I have this record at home...'

'But there's a rose in the fisted glove
'And the eagle flies with the dove
'And if you can't be with the one you love,
'Love the one you're with –'

'Well?'

'Well what?' he echoed.

'Well, if I have this record at home, then they must be good, mustn't they?' – She giggled as if cute, then (what it must've cost her in pride!) slipped a hand through his arm.

He froze. All the way over on the bench where I lurked, you could feel it. He stood there as if dumbstruck, or spellbound by the singers, or as if Dracula's sister had sunk her fangs in.

Her hand stayed hooked on his arm like a talon, until Seward swaggered onto the scene:

'Owe me a bottle, man. 'mazing dude. An' the boat – wow! Look, the guy's a friend a my friend Alistair. Told 'im I was with a chick so he told me to get her an' come back. You comin'?'

This was directed at Lydia, not me, who alone of the three he had spotted. But I was no more of interest to Seward than a half-pint of milk by that stage; he was on show to the rich at long last and needed some flash object to display, and Lydia in lamé was the sole candidate.

'What are you on about, Seward?' she managed, annoyed.

'Hey Lyddie, jus' thought you oughtta see what they're like… 'mericans in Europe with their shit together – I mean, not just backpackin' around blowin' weed n' puffin' flutes.'

This was said in the direction of the singers, who were countrified and out-of-place, but it applied to Tony and me too of course. She had long since scornfully noted how we were hardly the type to be done up in designer labels.

'What friend of what friend?' she inquired now, less intrigued by golddigging since the chance had arrived.

'Alistair. My friend in Monte Carlo. You know.'

'I didn't, as it happens. You hadn't dropped his name yet.'

'Alistair Moonchild.'

'Alistair whot?… sounds terribly dated and odd.'

'Come on, Lyddie' – Was there a threat in his tone? 'He's a little bit older, but age don't make no diff – 'cept that some folks get looser…' this with a sniff at Tony. 'Alistair knows what's hap'ning. Makes the world's best bullshot.'

'Best bullshit?' my man quipped; to which she laughed.

'Bullshot!' he corrected, being the one lampooned now.

'O deah… Well, Seward… but I do prefer drugs to spirits actually. Do you think we might score?'

Did Tony realize then that, for all her disparagement, she would have preferred him to any mythical yacht, Alistair or golddig? Could Seward see that she'd only been stringing him on to pay, score her toots and hedge her amorous bets with? Did his booze-sozzled brain have some insight under 'Ringadingdings'? Did his scowl at the prospect of having to go back to the yacht without 'chick' preview some latent urge for revenge?

'Score?' he echoed. 'Yeah, in Monte maybe; I can set it up. But Lyddie – ' he was offering her something that meant everything to him, *status*, and expected to be taken seriously now – 'that scene's a little more sophisticated than Camden Town. An' there might be one or two things better n' coke.'

'Better than coke?!' – She sounded incredulous.

'Sure,' he concluded. 'Come on.'

'That one, is it?' – She peered round at the boats.

'Naw, the next.'

'The next one? you mean that grey, ugly – '

'Lydia, that's no "grey, ugly" anything! That's the most far-out yacht I've ever seen!'

'Really...' With her hand still in Tony's arm, she decided (in truth, it was the last time she would have a choice). 'It's a bit late, Seward. Besides, one yacht's much the same as another, I suss. I fancy a coffee anyway. Fancy a coffee, Tony?... Have your gold-dig. We'll be in the Senaqweer.'

That decision, though not really hers to take, is one of the things that makes me wonder if she wasn't half in love with him in her own bizarre way. If so, poor Lydia! Because my man was an illusion in those days – maybe still is. No one could have had him, not really. He was like me almost, nearly unformed. Some sacrifice was needed to make us fully human, it seemed: some real blood of a kind.

Maybe she knew this on some subconscious level. Maybe that's part of what compelled us to her too: I wish I could ask. Anyhow, then they went on to the Senequier, busiest bar in the town, a place where a novice far drunker than I could have eavesdropped on people far soberer than they without being detected. Curiosity, or perverse admiration, had gotten the better of me. And what did I have to feel guilty for anyway? it wasn't as if I was reading his mail or stealing a peek at her diary. And if she was going to go after my man right there in public, why should I've been fussy about her privacy?

'If she isn't here by the time Seward gets back,' he was saying, 'I'll give you the keys.'

'Don't be daft. I don't drive anyway.'

The waiter came and did his thing. I was loitering behind what held up the awning.

'Look, I assure you she's just on a loon... You can't really imagine there's something you've done to deserve this... You know, I told her how beautiful it was, your relationship; how much I wished I had something like it. But I haven't found it yet.

And until I do, I just must stay on my own…'

She punctuated this speech with a satisfied slurp. I twisted to check out his reaction.

'Tony, I'm thirty – two,' she went on, 'and I've been through three scenes: one for five years, one for two and one for six – months. Scenes like yours – completely together, I mean – and, well, I've sussed a good many things in that time; and the most important is that, if it's not right – if it doesn't feel *all* right – then you simply must give up and go on your own.'

So here came the maternal chorus again. And she was good at it! touching that raw nerve. She even had you wondering for a spell if she wasn't just some older, wiser friend trying to help us fool kids to grow up.

'It was quite difficult to make that decision. The first time it took years – I was only twenty-odd, such a daft little cow; about Lauren's age, I should guess. I couldn't understand, *wouldn't* understand, why I was so unhappy. And then one morning, all of a sudden it was, I woke up to the realization that I'd done the right thing – the only right thing!… Then with the next one, I'd learned. Cooled it straightaway – almost, that is.'

Her cup hit its saucer. 'You told this to Lauren?'

'Yes, more or less. But Tony, you don't think… Look, if there *is* something up with her, well then perhaps it's meant to – perhaps… yes. Yes, I hadn't seen till now: there *is* something, isn't there? Yes, I hadn't sussed it before. O, I'd noticed little things: how she's a bit more sensitive than you in ways you don't understand, feels things that you cahn't because you're so – factual sometimes. And sometimes you can be so maddeningly silent and into yourself; in some ways, I don't think you understand women at all. And then there's that trip about marriage, which you claim to have worked out but – '

'I didn't realize you were that old.'

How cruel we could be! – 'Yes, Tony. I'm thirty – two. And I've been through… O it's so difficult to find that, that – '

I twisted the other way, trying to catch her expression.

'No, it's all right,' she sniffed at him, 'I know…' and laying a hand on his arm: 'One must spend years getting to know oneself before…' Brandishing a pink kleenex, she blew a trumpeting note. 'By the time I reach forty perhaps…'

'Forty?!' – He drew back like he'd been stung by a wasp.

'O I know it sounds an age to you, but something will turn up – yes, I'm sure it will; that's one thing I have never doubted; I seem to know it intuitively. I have faith, and… O Tony, don't you think maybe you've been with her for the wrong reasons? I mean, you're so beautifully young still and have so much –'

That was enough. I slipped from behind my post and around the tables, back to the front of the place and up to them. Flouncing my hair out and unlacing my halter, I made as if I'd just I'd just swirled in off a wave of breathless excitement.

'Where've you been?' he demanded, shooting up.

Ignoring him completely, I crowed at her: 'What a trip, Lyddie! – Moroccan, not French. Just like a black American jive-artist: rap rap rap about everything, and laughed? Shit, what a fantastic loon! You missed it. What happened?'

Recoiling, she drilled her dark eyes into mine. Could she tell by some sixth sense that I'd overheard everything?

'And you mimicked every bit, did you?'

'Rap rap right back – in French yet! What a trip!'

Tony was trying to put an arm around me. Wriggling free, I bounded away, as if I had no more interest in him. And in that moment I felt as if I held them both in my palm; and the sense of control was delicious. But already you could see her plotting her next move – 'Yes,' she muttered, 'I'll bet you loved it.'

It would take me years still to realize how much her kind of power was backed up by little more than a diminutive female's fragile nerve.

*

Sex was a habit between him and me by then, a narcotic trying to stop up a void that only maturity or authority could fill. His hands would move over my secret places abstractly; I'd turn away. So what would happen? To my misery, he would just paw and breast-stroke till he had a hard-on and then go ahead even if I lay there like a corpse.

I didn't come with him anymore. Did he notice? Wordless, he'd roll off leaving me to wonder if he'd ever really given a shit about how I felt. Stretched out there beside him, I'd doze finally. Then I'd be lying awake and meditating on the stars sparkling like pixie-dust over Ste Maxime.

Their light was profuse, like in the desert at night. A three-quarter moon was pouring its silver over the flagstones, glittering the gravel along the drive. The fig-bush, oleander and ancient barn at the turn of the road all stood out hyper-distinct, moon-washed, looking as if they could transform on a whim into animate, avenger presences.

Something could happen here in these hills, I fantasized. Disaster could arrive, and who would know? Lying there opening myself up to the strangeness, I saw a primitive stare coming of the dark, its mouth loose, its teeth jagged, its eyes cut by red rage. I tried to turn from it, this face from a nightmare; still, I gazed as if dumbstruck. Then I knew where I'd seen it – in the afternoons, driving back from the beach: it was the face of the old farmer at the turn in the road. He'd been there all the time, as if to warn us. So was he like some surreal version of the authority-figure we'd gone off looking for?

Out in the thickets, wind moaned. It murmured morosely, laced with dog whines. Under the moon's spell, the whines echoed; then there'd be silence – no sound but that tireless breath of a breeze, ancient bringer of wonder and dream, of fear and phantasm, a whisper voicing tales out of Arab and Greek, Phoenician and Jew, Roman and so on, lullaby-ing you as you fell back into non-entity…

I was wandering through a real vision of Tony and cars, Lydia and me and someone else in deepening illusion when I felt a presence creeping toward us. In half-sleep I heard it scrape at the shutters, then sigh. Starting up, I strained to roll my eyes into blackness and saw a shape hovering at the foot of our bed.

Kicking out, I felt it flinch, then saw it retreat, vague as a shadow from some nameless world.

I was wide awake then. I could feel a sensation of bones on my toes. Tony shifted, draping an arm over my breast... It had been no illusion, no. Nor was I sleepwalking when I got up to close the doors against the possibility of a thief in the night.

In the morning Seward and Lydia announced they were going to leave us for the heights of would-be-dom: their mythical 'Monte'. They needed us now only to get them there. So, down the coast we rattled in our humble Beetle, Tony being too 'mean' to take the péage.

Ste Maxime, St Raphaël – we gazed at the sources of light we had stared at from the patio as suns set over the Golfe. Esterel, the clay towers, gleaming sapphire sea; then Cannes – too much traffic; Antibes, Juan-les-Pins... T and S had a dispute about where Fitzgerald and Hemingway had 'hung out'; Lydia contented herself with fantasies involving famous names and glam affairs. Finally, in a lather, we arrived in Nice and were fighting crazy traffic along the Promenade des Anglais. Deciding against checking the mail at Amex – too many straw hats, back-packs and Topeka accents – we pressed on in our rattle-bug, just tuned by Seward, till it was swerving behind sleek wheels down the route of the Grand Prix.

Fabled Monaco: pristine yachts, pristine harbour, pristine promenade... Apartment towers, soaring corniche...

'Look!' Seward enthused, adrenalin racing in anticipation of *the* meeting. 'Gus said Alistair'd be at the Beach Club. What're you two gonna do?'

Tony and I glanced at each other. Were we really so unpresentable that we couldn't be seen?

'I'm taking a swim,' said my man and, parking the car abruptly, headed off for the water.

'I'll go to the Club, see if he's there. I'd say come along, but... Wanna come, Lyddie, or – ?'

He snitched her pocket mirror to slick back a hair; she eyed him dubiously. Fuck them, I thought and followed Tony to spread out on some miniature boulders pretending to be sand.

'I think I'll stay with this lot,' I heard her murmur in belated, unexpected loyalty to us.

He snorted as if she'd made a rash decision, but without further comment he traipsed away, leaving her to come settle down next to me.

This was with more than the usual ceremoniousness. So was she having mild coke withdrawals, or was there something else causing her to fidget with fags and so on? I didn't ask; she didn't offer. We were keeping it to ourselves today.

After a time, Tony resurfaced from a pale lip of sea.

'Seward's excited,' he commented, shaking out his hair.

'You've sussed that, have you?'

'What do you think this Alistair's going to be like?'

'I should think he'll be just what Seward fancies being in twenty years time, only...' She exhaled. 'Shull miss you lot, you know. I expect I'll find this scene a bit of a drag.'

Was this genuine affection, or just stage fright?

'You'll only be here a few days,' he observed.

'Yes but... O I must get back to London; the're so many things I've let go. When are you two coming back by the way?'

I looked to Tony, who looked to me. 'Quien sabe.'

'I'll expect a visit in any case, when you arrive.'

We had hardly a minute to weigh the significance of this before Seward had reappeared: 'He's waiting with the car, man! Invited us all up for a drink!'

'All of us?'

'Yup. Come on!' – He was breathless.

'Like this?' – Sandy bikinis and cutoffs for *the* meeting? There was more than a touch of irony in our tone.

''s cool,' he assured, as if in complete control. 'Come on, man: hurry up! Can't keep 'em waiting...'

So that's how we came to clap eyes on the magical Alistair and friend. They were leaning against an Italian sports car by the promenade, Alistair bald, pale, paunchy, middle-aged and wear-

ing a red playsuit, red gold-buckled shoes and red-rimmed darkglasses, while the friend was tanned, ageless, sexless and dressed
in a black caftan, black slippers, jet-rimmed darkglasses and a
toupee of Roman Empire bangs.

'Here they are – God! May I present Terry, Lydia, Samantha,
Carol, Babs, André, Oscar and the rest of the hippy cherubs.
This is Caesar Augusta.'

'Gus actually,' the friend said, in tainted English.

Self-consciousness seeped from us thick as the scent of
Coppertone. Cramming into the back of their Iso Griffo or whatever, we sped through gilded streets listening to our host quote
from 'that Manhattan bitch Capote' about what he thought of
'hippy mentality'.

Seward guffawed and provided set-ups: 'Hey Alistair, remember the time we took the Rolls an' – '

'Do I remember? God, the hours I spent trying to think what
to do with him – it, I mean. It was too obvious to park in front,
too tempting to put in the garage and this cad was afraid the
Monegasques'd thieve his Flying Lady if he left her at the servants' entrance, which is the only safe place. As it was, he made a
public spectacle of unscrewing her each time he blessed us with
his seraphic face.'

'Unscrewing her?!' Lydia echoed.

'Isn't that what I said, dear?'

Seward chortled. 'So what're you up to these days, 'listair?'

'What am I "up to"? God! When Gus told me he'd called, I
went to the Club, picked out the cushiest chair under the widest
umbrella, put on the darkest pair of darkglasses I could thieve,
draped *Le Monde* over my face, ordered six gin-and-tonics, and
tried to pretend I was dead.'

'I just looked for all the empties, haha!'

'Do you know this cad? God! I wish I could say I didn't. The
only reason I put up with him is he's marrying into the family.'

'Marrying into the family?!'

'Isn't that what I said, dear?'

Seward turned sheepish. 'Haven't seen her for a while, Al.

Last time I did, she was on a pretty weird trip.'

'O? and where was she going?'

'No "trip",' Lydia translated. 'State of mind.'

Alistair wheeled on her. 'I may look like granddad to you, but I do comprehend the language – God! A sexual trip, I should hope. Her father wanted a boy, and my sister had the enlightenment to call her "Gay". But this all-American cad is going to unscrew-her-up for us, aren't you neph? When's the happy day?'

Seward chortled. The rest of us squirmed.

There was no doubt why our rich-kid friend had been reluctant to bring Tony, or at least me, to meet him. Alistair was a savage posing as being civilized. Unlike us, he was formed, which made him fascinating. Unlike Lydia even, he had a hard core: principles, or lack of them, absolute and repellent. He had turned waywardness into a code, which made him despise us, who hadn't. It also made you wonder, subconsciously, if *he* wasn't the real authority-figure we had set out looking for.

His apartment was on the eleventh floor, overlooking the harbour. 'The Casino's up there, and Grace's place there – the palace to you kids – and – which? that long white thing with the masts on it? belongs to... No, I haven't been on that one – God, who does that lovely piece belong to? Or is that the one Piero went to St Tropez on last week?'

Antiques, Impressionist oils, Oriental objets... 'I used to deal seriously but got rather bored...' Monstrous house-plants, gushes of ivy, gilt-bound first editions... 'God, that girl has lovely hair!' – He patted a fatty palm against my cheek. 'Have you ever seen such luxurious locks?'

Lydia was not having this. 'Where's the Grand Prix route then?' – She pronounced it 'pricks', naturally.

Alistair nodded to Gus while continuing to gaze at my hair, as if reverent. 'This pied-noir can give you the facts.' – Seeing who constituted the weight in our foursome, he was already calculating how to deal with her.

'Hey Alistair,' chirped Seward. 'Howsa 'bout a bullshot?'

41

'Is he going to remind me? God! But he did learn something about the art of drunking when he was here. A case of consommé in – what was it? three days? Fortunately, he stole sufficient good breeding to send a replacement; otherwise, he would never've been allowed through Uncle Ally's front door again.'

'Really?' – Lydia waved a cigarette, soliciting a match.

'She's a bit haughty, this one. Tell me, dear' – he snapped a torch underneath it – 'where're you from? The Bronx?'

'The Bronx?!'

'Isn't that what I said?'

Poor Lyddie. She was too proud not to rise to the bait:

'I'm afraid you're quite wrong. I'm English, as it happens.'

'Ah. That explains it.'

'Explains whot?'

'The bored heiress bit. But which part of Fair Albion is it? Or no, shall I guess? Yes, that might amuse you... The West, shall we say. The Black Country?'

'The Black Country?!'

'Isn't that what I said?'

'In actual point of fact' – she puffed her torso up to the peak of its pertness – 'I am from London. I should've thought anyone who knew would've known. I've never in my life been taken for one of those... others.'

'I know London well, dear. I lived there for thirteen years, off the King's Road. Perhaps it's these uncultured colonials who've dulled your accent; though not your charming wit.' – He turned to Tony abruptly, asking, 'Is she with you, or – ?'

Allergic to the type, my man ignored him.

Seward in the meantime started to bray, 'Hey 'listair, what about that bullshot?'

'Who is that cad? God! Didn't he learn a thing the last time? A bullshot's a morning drink.'

''s only about six. Still morning to you, ha!'

Our host looked around in dismay. 'What've we done to deserve it? God! Well, I won't compound the bad taste by refusing. Gus, could you? Strong, I think.'

Like a genie evaporating from a bottle, the pied-noir wafted out of the room. We all stared after him.

Alistair seemed amused:

'You think he's a ghoul? Imagine when I found him – detention camp, end of the war. Injected new life into him, gave him a name, taught him to speak, made him a man again.'

No one dared touch this.

'What is a pied-noir?' I asked.

'But why, my angel, would you want to fill that adorable head with such a useless old fact?' – The palm patted my cheek damply. 'You have such beautiful colour. You all have such lovely colours – as if you belonged to some new southern race. Escaped our dead northern whiteness at last.'

This seemed a cue for Lydia to re-enter. 'But I'm afraid I shall peel!' she said, pulling back her robe.

'Look!' he mock-whispered. 'Children, will you just… lovely! She's nearly showing her… Really, dear. Perfect!'

'It's so sore!'

'Stay exactly like that, I have just the thing…'

He smoothed out and, before she could make a behind-the-hand dig, returned with a small, gilt-and-blue-enamel box. This he presented with a flourish, opening the lid on a cream-coloured ointment. Peering at it curiously, she daubed a fingertip.

'How come you're so white, Al?' Seward meanwhile asked.

'Have to save the sun for you tourists.'

He guffawed. Lydia sniffed a finger.

'That's it, dear. Just dab it on and smear it over.'

Feeling all eyes on her, the queen-bee did just that.

'God! Will you look? Children, lovely! Piero came with it. I'm afraid the poor boy holds all the answers, if he only knew…'

No one inquired what that was supposed to mean.

'Does it really stop peeling?' she demanded, self-absorbed.

'Just rub it in, dear; cures all petty burns. I wouldn't want any of my remarks to rub you the wrong way.'

Seward, still spluttering over 'sun for the tourists', shot off on a new roller-coaster of mirth.

Lydia for her part now became dead-set on keeping all attention on a body she imagined to be her invincible trump-card. Alistair hovered on edge, his smile as changeless as the ambiguous tone of his words. All she had over him in this battle of bitches was looks and youth, but both were blown away like so many feathers the moment his boy slouched in.

'Ah. Piero. So… you heard us.'

From some inner sanctum he emerged yawning, as if just waking from deepest sleep. Piero was eighteen perhaps: dark, lean in the chest and the leg. His eyes were sunken in coal-circled sockets. They seemed like they might flash to life as they wandered over us but went dull instead and settled gradually on the toes of his Italian-sandaled feet.

'You remember this cad?' – The tone petted and mocked at the same time; Piero glanced at Seward and shook his head.

It seemed against his will to remember. It seemed against his will to be there at all, dressed up so prettily in white linen, pleated trousers and a baby-blue V-neck.

'Piero…' Alistair drew out the name. 'This is Piero, the other half of the story; force of the future, if he could only wake up. Eh, Piero? Piero, sit. Meet the bronzed children: this is Tony – Laurie – and – what did you say her name was? Your brothers and sisters, Piero. Say hi.'

The boy stood rigid by a Louis XV sideboard. 'I have just now been – how you say – sleepy?'

'Sleeping, yes. I'm teaching Piero how to speak. As you can see, he's a bit confused…'

Master eyed minion. The rest of us sat there wearing the rinds of impossible smiles. We were in Alistair's dominion, not Camden Town, as Seward had said; Alistair could do as he liked here, no matter who else did. I for one didn't and was ready to leave; Tony was too, you could see. It was only a social version of what Seward would call 'entropy' that held us.

Gus wafted back in with a tray holding six glasses and a pitcher of blood-coloured liquid. Under cover of this, or maybe in hopes of hiding, Piero gravitated toward the most unobtrusive of the guests.

'Are you Italian?' I asked when he sat next to me.

'I am Tunisian.'

'Is Piero a Tunisian name?'

But Alistair was not having his boy to get intimate with anyone, not even someone so unthreatening:

'We thought it an appropriate tag, didn't we? No, Piero's
one of Gus' discoveries, angel. Arab for the most part: American
only by recent injections.'

'Bullshots!' Seward had the grace to explete.

'Is this cad still here? God, nephew, get drunk! Yes, do something for pity's sake.'

On our way back to St Trop, Tony would remark that if you
were a painter you could sum the guy up by throwing a few
blobs of red and black at a canvas already sponged over in pink.
Brilliant and terrifying as he was to begin with, Alistair ended by
seeming like some dull magus or wicked prince leading his dev-
otees down to a ritual in the murk. Seward zoomed through two
pitchers of bullshots as if at a race ('Fast starters, late finishers'
would be Tony's phrase) and by the third was terminally woozy.
Lydia had grown completely limp-wrested by the time she was
attempting to wave Gus away.

'Is something the matter?' our host inquired, brows arched.

'I prefer other things, thanks.'

'"Other things"? What sort of things? I have everything you
could possibly imagine, I'm sure.'

'Do you?'

'Isn't that what I said? Do you think I'm known as the gayest
of blades this side of the East River on looks alone?'

She should have had the sense to desist. But Lydia would
continue to try to shit long after unsophisticates like Tony and
myself had got off the pot.

'When you put it like that,' she slurred, looking him down,
'I suppose not.'

Alistair's smile went from false to malicious. 'You know, if it
weren't for the fact that this jerk might marry into the family, I'd

throw every one of you out without so much as a coke!'

'"Coke", did you say?'

'Dear lady, pointing out that you'll never find a better-equipped host than an American expatriate, nor a more complete supply of liquor than Alistair Moonchild's – '

'"Licker?!"' she mimicked. 'I'm afraid I gave that up some time ago. I've found there're much hipper things, thanks.'

'Ah. I begin to understand… Piero: what do we have to fix the lady up with?'

'No goddam thing!'

'Piero…' A stroking moment of silence. 'You see, dear, these "hipper things", as you call them, are quite often expensive. And since poor Piero doesn't have a sou to his name…'

'Bullshots!' Seward had the inane timing to resound.

'So it would appear.' – She sighed. 'Well, if I am condemned to drink them, I should like to know at least how they're made.'

'You take vodka – ' Alistair.

'Smirnoff's!' – Seward.

'Consommé – '

'Campbell's!'

'And – '

'Woostersheer Sauce, an' – '

'Woster Sauce,' she corrected.

'That's what I said, an' – '

'No you said "Worstersheer".'

'But we colonials never knew how to speak. What is your sign, dear? Cancer? Please tell us. And Gus, could you possibly…' He waved at the pitcher. 'A touch more fatal this time, I think.'

The ghoul wafted out.

'One, two, three, four – God! What've I done? I'm charitable to one poor cad and now I have four. Be charitable to them and – eight, twelve, sixteen? I'll have to be a shit.'

While Seward erupted, Lydia considered Alistair as if coolly, though by now she was too bleary to keep up much pretence. Tony's gaze had travelled to the stars through the windows, so I turned to Piero to try to draw him out. Master, however, had at last had enough:

'He can't speak, dear.' – Grasping the boy by the neck, he literally threw him toward the door through which Gus had vanished, proving, lest you had any doubt, that he was not just verbally menacing, but violent and, though flabby, no wimp.

Piero disposed of, he turned to us:

'All the hippy cherubs... utterly dumbstruck suddenly?'

Lydia was finished, or seemed so.

Toward Seward, he sneered: 'Cat got the tongue, nephew?' Putting hands on his hips, he soliloquised to Gus, who'd resurfaced, 'What shall we do now? teach them to speak? But what could they tell us? what do they know nowadays? They have pills now, not war: birth control, "other things". And what do they do on them? wander from one beauty-spot to another looking for – Ha!' He turned with a flourish. 'How unutterably fed-up I am!' – On which note, he exited.

4.

Bad vibrations, bad driving, headache, moon and cloud... Had the period of no fun started? the phase of growing up really?

I flipped in and out of dreams, premonitions of guilt. I heard Tony get up but couldn't face him. He was hovering, kissing my lids. Pretending to be asleep, I turned away from the day.

With the sheet over my head, I flip-flopped some more, until it was too bright, too hot. Kicking it back, I hid my eyes in the pillow, which was sopping wet.

People came to me – old friends, parents, people I could love and learn from, they said. Should we go home, I asked. But what would he tell me? what think? What was he thinking? And where had he gone so early in the day?

Out on the stones, dog nails clicked.

'Viens chienne... viens ici.' – She stood in the door, tongue lolling, tail wagging weakly; then, as if coming to a happy decision, she lowered her muzzle and pattered in.

Licking my face, she nuzzled up like a lover. But something was wrong, some noise in the distance. I twisted in half-dream: there was an attack, a struggle; at last no more sound; then a scratch, scratch at the door – 'Chienne?' – then no scratching... an irregular patter; a faint moan, as if whine, far away.

I got out of bed and unbolted the storm-door. There was blood on the tiles – not just a spot, but profusion smeared in paw prints. The prints crossed the gravel and disappeared into the brush blocking the garbage-pit from view. Other prints crossed the gravel and passed out of sight by the far end of the villa.

I went back through our room and out the patio door. At the edge of the stones my bitch stood.

Blood dripped from her neck. 'Chienne!'

She hovered there trying to drag herself toward me. One of her forelegs was torn open from thigh down.

'Chienne!' – She stumbled on three legs. 'Viens ici!' I murmured and, taking her by the scruff, led her into the shade of our shutters. I forced her to lie.

Desperate, she licked at the dirtied gash, bloodying her muzzle. The flow wouldn't stop; as if embarrassed, she licked at the pool it made on the stones.

'Pauvre chienne!' – stroking matted hair, 'pauvre chienne, reste ici...' I ran inside, collected soap, iodine and one of Tony's t-shirts to rip into bandages. Emptying a wine bottle, I filled it with water and came back out.

A trail of blood led from the pool to the last door on the patio, which was open. The dog was at the foot of the Frenchman who, naked as Adam, was crouching to study her wound. She licked at the fresh pool she made.

'Du sang,' he muttered, hearing me come.

'Oui. La blessure. Elle a perdu – '

'Beaucoup du sang, si. L'autre côté aussi. Tiens.'

Without hesitation he took the shirt from my hand and,

tearing it into strips, began to wrap her leg.

I finished washing her wounds.

We worked together in silence.

'How do you think it happened?' I asked after a time.

'They come. They fight; perhaps one, perhaps many. I saw a black dog in the brush. Perhaps c'est lui.'

It was not until he had finished that he looked up. 'Tu es gentille,' he said and, seeming only then to notice he was nude, added, 'Excuse-moi – tu resteras avec elle?'

He went in.

The dog's heart throbbed. Her eyes were deep circles of brown, as warm as his skin. The throb went at a wild pace; 'Chienne…' My mind was still focused on this new imprint, just absent beside me. 'No no, chienne.'

Taking her muzzle away from the bandage, she panted and lapped at the blood oozing with fretful slaps of the tongue. Sighing, she laid her head on the stones.

In the meantime, a scrap of paper fluttering out of my door rose and floated down on a breeze:

My love –
Gone to Pamplonne. Yr asleep and I imagine after last
night you need yr rest. Meet me à la plage when yr up.
                                                    – T.

The Frenchman came back out wearing his red bun-huggers. We carried the bitch to the corner by my door; there was shade there and would be still till the sun came around the house in the mid-afternoon.

Her paps swung low against my arms as we set her down. 'Isn't there anything else we can do?'

Squatting on the doorstep, he shrugged.

'There is no one she belongs to?'

'Elle est libre sans doute.'

'But there must be some organization to take her.'

He shrugged again, less indifferent this time.

'Je vais aux autres villas et demander!' I declared.

He put a hand over his eyes and squinted up at me. 'Il ne faut pas faire cela.'

'But something has to be done!' – I felt a surge of teenaged bravado and, against his protest, set off...

Brush picked and ripped at the hem of my nightie. Flushed with false courage, I thought: even if he doubts my judgement, he'll be impressed by my spirit.

At the first villa, no one. At a second, no one answered though a car in the drive had disgorged its keys onto a kitchen table. At a third, a modern one, I came up to the porch so softly that the four playing bridge there didn't notice till I was standing over them. 'Sacré nom!' one exclaimed at this apparition in white. I explained myself as well I could but, whether because of my French or out of genuine ignorance, they offered no advice.

At last I came to the house at the turn of the road. The old farmer stared at me with eerie grisliness, until I remembered the face in my dream. By then, my adrenalin rush was exhausted and I was ready to go back to base.

'Ca, c'est futile,' the Frenchman remarked, still in the same spot, waiting for me.

'But the're other villas. Up in the hills, I'll try them.'

'You should not.' – He smoked.

'Pourquoi pas?'

'Because... inutile. Besides, you are a woman. You should not wander dans les endroits étranges.'

'But I will!' – I turned to go; he caught me by the wrist.

'Non!' – Then more softly: 'J'y vais.'

A little knife twisted as he went back to his chamber – could it be that I actually want to go in there with him? 'Chienne, pauvre chienne,' I intoned, stroking the beast. Then he came back out, in sandals and darkglasses, looking like an advertisement off some glossy magazine.

He vanished through the oleanders. We waited, the bitch and I. At one point, she woofed, attempting to stand; I followed her eyes to see movement in the brush. 'Allez!' – At the edge of the drive, a young black hound nosed forward. 'Allez!' – Cocking an ear, he sniff-sniffed beyond me toward blood. 'Allez!' – No other dog being good now, I picked up a handful of gravel and threw it to drive him away.

The bitch had wobbled up to sniff his direction. 'Reste là, chienne,' I murmured as a gust crossed the stones knocking her into the wall. 'Lie down, girl; lie…' Muzzle confused in the air, she had to be calmed. 'No more wind now, it's OK…' At last, I'd resettled her onto her side, to watch as the sun arced the house, reached west and shone down on us directly. Then a station wagon came spitting stones up the drive, and my Frenchman and the sharp-haired landlady got out.

Sweat gleamed on their foreheads. Both were grimacing.

'Où est-elle?' the woman demanded.

'Là-bas.'

'Is she the dog's master?' I whispered to him.

'Ah, vous êtes ici,' she meanwhile said to the bitch. 'Qu'est-ce que tu as fait maintenant, chienne?'

The poor thing gazed at her in a daze of blankness.

'She is the agent,' he said. 'Monsieur le maître n'est pas ici.'

The landlady plucked at the bandage. Blood again oozed.

'Ne fais pas cela!' he commanded, startling me.

'You can keep the bandage,' I offered as she tried to pick up the burden.

'Vous êtes gentille, ma'moiselle, trop gentille,' she muttered, nearly dropping it.

'Here, let me help.'

'No, no, vous êtes trop gentille!' – Clutching it around the belly and squeezing the paps, 'No no, s'il vous plait, ouvrez la porte…' She lugged it like an overfilled suitcase to the wagon and dumped it in back. 'Vous êtes trop gentille…' Jamming the legs in as if bits of stray laundry, 'Monsieur vous remercie…' She slammed the tailgate shut.

'Will she be OK?'

'Vous êtes trop gentille.' – She glanced from me to the man I had assumed till that moment was French. 'Alors, bonne soirée,' she concluded with irony.

'Good night to you et Monsieur le maître aussi,' he shot back and, under his breath, 'Mme Juive!'

The woman shrugged. 'Algériens!' she muttered in kind and, getting into her driver's seat, spun the wagon down the drive spitting pebbles back at us.

A silence.

As if to himself, he mused: 'He has her puppies. He will use one, perhaps, to hunt or as watchdog; the others will have to wander like her, become old and enceinte. More puppies and then – ' Another gust of wind slapped in. 'When I told him she was comme ça...?' He shrugged, and expectorated. 'These types, they are without feeling.'

Now a blast of wind came. The slam of a door made me jump and look back toward Tony's and my room.

'Maintenant nous aurons le mistral,' he observed.

'Comment?'

'Ce vent. Regarde. It comes from the north down the valley of the Rhône; it turns aux Bouches and comes toward St Tropez. It may stay one day or three days or five. C'est mauvais pour tout – shakes the doors, makes the sounds in the night. Et puis, il n'y a plus de paix.'

Only a few gusts had hit Pamplonne by the time I got there. A few timid sunbathers – or maybe they were veterans who'd recognized the prelude – found reason to pack up for their villas. The rest seemed to forget in the stillness that followed. No one seemed ready for a Mistral.

Profound eeriness lurked, preparing to strike. Stray clothes came to life and surrealistically raced out to sea. Bodies chased towels or stumbled trying to step into shifts. A piece of *Le Monde* flew up, enwrapped a man's leg, tore away. An umbrella took flight, hitting a second man in the eye; his wife started to scream as she saw blood course down his cheek.

'Ma petite?' a mother cried, bustling past. 'Où es-tu, ma petite?'

I searched for Tony. Yachts raced from Tahiti plage back to the harbour; rental sloops swamped; rafts surfed on reversed waves out to rescue.

'Ma petite! Où es-tu?'

The cables of beached boats stroked one another, sending up wails. 'Au mistral!' one faithful nudist cried, popping a cork and raising a bottle to the stormy west. And it *was* impressive, the prospect: so full of high drama that it almost did seem to call for a toast, which is what Tony must have been thinking, wherever he was.

A cloudbank masked the sun. The wind turned cold and rushed across the sand like some laughing marauder. Human cries rose, mixed with cable whines. Even the faithful began to get dressed now and flee. It was as if some mad army or furious beast had been set loose against us.

Sand swirled, stinging faces. Panic hovered, mean as Alistair's tongue. Off the beach went the French and Belgians and Germans; I started to run back along Route des Plages against the wind in slow-motion. Refugee cars passed; voices cat-called. So what if I had a big American 'bum', I jeered back. Fuck all you self-indulgent Euro-creeps!

Legs-muscles tightened, the wind fighting every pace. Slap-slap went my tennies till I was bent over, throwing up, retching, cursing our days of drink and drugs and smoke; collapsing against a vineyard wall, wind drying my sweat, blown drops of spit on my chin making me think of myself as a version of that sweet, dying bitch with the wounds in her neck...

'Viens, méchant!' a guttural voice sounded.

Loping by the old farmhouse, I saw a black apparition in the road in front of me. Its hackles rising like razor blades, it bared its teeth and was making a weird, plaintive moan, like a hunchback about to strangle his faithless, pretty young wife.

'Viens, méchant!' the ancient farmer repeated and, coming out from behind a crumble of wall, yanked the creature back by the scruff of the neck and, whacking it over the muzzle, threw it in one and the same motion into a barn.

I carried on.

'Lauren?' The doors rattled. 'Lauren, are you there?' – Rattle, rattle. 'Lauren, if you're in there, why're the doors locked?'

Wearily I got up, pulled the bolt and lay back.

He was lingering on the step, a silhouette against a sky across which clouds thundered en masse. To the west, there was one small rent in this tapestry; through it, red-orange oozed.

'Haven't you gotten up all day?' he asked.

I didn't know what to say, so I didn't.

'What's this mess?' – He squinted at blood on the stones.

'I tried to find you,' I managed.

'Didn't you get my note?' – He stepped around it and in.

'Yeah. I went to the beach. But couldn't find you.'

'Hmm… OK. Listen to this…'

Flopping down beside me, he began:

> 'Exhaling spirit
> 'Driving to shelter
> '(– to inhale after,
> 'Drawing out, upward):
>
> 'Bright-driving,
> 'Night-moaning,
> 'Storm-haired
> 'Glitter-chaser…'

'But Tony, it's awful.'

'What's awful?'

'It's so eerie and violent. I don't like the feelings I'm getting here.'

'But it's so – dramatic! all that black and gold and blood-red smeared against grey – look!'

He pushed back the door to show the rip in the clouds: it had expanded into a wide swath. Then his foot hit on something. Leaning down – small, hard, round: what was it he picked up?

'Excuse me,' my Algerian said suddenly, appearing out of the sky beside him. 'I have left my... Ah: you have found it. Merci.'

He took a lighter from Tony's hand.

Silence. Wind slapping the walls...

'Elle est morte maintenant sans doute,' the man went on, looking in at me obliquely.

Tony hadn't budged from the door.

I nodded in vagueness.

'We must wash this,' he added, dropping his eyes.

A gust of silence.

'Alors, le vent est fâché. You must shut the doors...' Having observed thus, he disappeared.

Tony turned to me:

'What's been happening here, Lauren?'

'Don't touch me now, please.'

'What did you say?'

'I think maybe we ought to go home.'

He hovered there in the half-light. I pulled my hand free.

'A dog,' I began in part explanation. 'The landlady killed it.'

He gazed at sunset for several seconds. Finally, as if making up his mind, he shut the doors and lay down next to me.

'OK so you're upset. But you know, these things happen in life. We're not at home now; we can't pretend to know what's right here and wrong, it's a different country... Hey, don't do this now...' He touched a hand to my cheek: he was trying so hard to be kind. 'You wanna go into town? have a nice dinner?'

I said, 'It's not that different here.'

'What?'

'Right and wrong here from right and wrong anywhere. The richer you are the righter, and they're pigs and racists just as much as Alistair and – '

'Look Lauren, we can't let our lives be fucked up by somebody else's trip. I mean, we got the loaded-n-looners out of the way; now maybe we can have something for the two of us.'

It was about time he came up with that – but so late!

He took off his cutoffs and spooned against me. Slipping

his hand round my tummy, he started to rub. It was gentle and steady, like the way I used to stroke my Alsatian when lying beside it in front of TV. Blowing into my ear, he kissed it. You could feel him get hard.

'Hey,' he muttered finally, 'you just gonna lie here all night... like you did all fucking day?'

It wasn't an accusation, though the implication was there. 'I want to get out of this place,' is all I answered.

His hardon subsided. The bed slowly rose.

'What does that mean?'

'It means, I want to get out of Europe.'

He pulled his jeans up. 'You're being childish, Lauren.'

'Well, what's the point?' – Propping myself against the pillow, I went on, 'I'm not doing anything; you're not doing anything... Today you wrote some song lyric – so? You've started a half dozen songs since we left California; what does that do for anyone? What are we doing, other than wandering from one scene to another looking for – '

'Shut up and get dressed.'

'No!... don't feel like it.'

'Come on,' he said, coaxing. 'Why be like this?'

'Because I'm sick of it, man. Sick to death!' – And twisting angrily back to the pillow, I buried my face.

'All right... if that's how you want it. I'll go to town by myself and get dinner by myself, and you can wallow in your bleeding heart or go moon with your frog prince or go home to America and do what you fucking well please, Lauren; because I don't give a shit, Lauren. When I do a trip, I do it all the way, whether I like what everyone else's doing or not. But you – you're just too fucking, self-righteously childish to see that... there's two of us here, you know, and we can't always be holding each other back from – O I don't know. Maybe we *have* been together for the wrong reasons!'

The sun in its death-throes had opened the sky. Clouds were moving out to sea, the wind blowing in and through town without rest. The promenade was swept clean; stray walkers moved intently to shelter, eastward on winged feet, westward in cartoon-like slow-motion.

The harbour was overcrowded with ghost yachts – mass exodus to terra firma. In front of the cafés, chairs and tables sat in confused barricade. Restaurants were shuttered, service impatient. Business was no pleasure in a mistral.

Big cars sped by mindless; tiny 2CVs imitated unsteadily. At the kerb by the Papagayou, a usual retinue of hitchhikers had vanished. Where had this ill-wind blown them?

I was swept into a brightly lit, untrendy place we'd never gone to with Seward and Lydia. It wasn't shuttered or readied for battle like the others but full of locals, some even having pleasure still. At the very back, I saw his shaggy head bobbing while he cleared a plate. I longed to go there, make up and have things like they'd been; but some jealous spirit breathed that it wasn't my orange hair or pleasingly plump body he wished were sitting with him. And how can you just go racing over to some guy you imagine is dreaming about somebody else?

In front of a deserted bar, a teenaged boy declared to the American street-singing couple, who bravely tried to perform: 'Il faut que vous attaquiez les Français!'

'Sorry, bro?' the male of the pair inquired.

'Il faut que vous attaquiez les Français!'

This teenager was one of a group of three dressed in tight jeans and leathers. The American had long hair and wore overalls; his girl was in a granny dress.

'Mais il faut!' the French boy insisted, his friends seconding him – it was like a tableau of European vs American hip: 'Attaquez les Français, les Anglais, les Américains et tout le monde trop riche ici... dans les restaurants et bateaux, appartements et tout ces places comme cela, attaquez! comme Bob Dylan avec les Américains – il le faut!'

Having vented this spleen, he and his comrades moved on, leaving the couple to shrug. 'I ain't attackin' or bein' attacked, 'f I kin help it,' the male muttered, packing his instrument and setting it on the bench I had wandered over to sit on. His girl meanwhile went a circuit of the bar, tambourine in hand.

At this moment, a second couple burst out of l'Escale down the promenade. The female of the pair was bottle-blonde, bottle-tanned and elegant in a couturier trouser-suit, with enough gold to support the singers for a year. The man was six-foot, wearing Gucci loafers and a shirt opened to expose chest hair and a silver coke-spoon – an aging rich kid with a Sunbelt twang.

Her accent was British. 'But don't you see?' she asked. 'I was the one who had to take all that hateful, horrid attack! I've never in my life been spoken to like that.'

'Talk's cheap, babe.' – His words were smeared from copious booze.

'Yes, and now we don't even have the price of a coffee... O if I only had gone with Nigel: *he* would have stood up for me. But you, you... O I know you would've if you could've, darling. But at least we're alone now – I don't care about anything else so long as – '

They passed on into the Senequier.

'Far out, man!' the male of the singing pair chuckled.

'What was that about?' I asked.

'Season gits overripe here mighty quick. Floey's right – time for us to be movin' on. Been livin' a dream.'

Floey, his girl, had returned, tambourine nearly empty. 'We did 'merikin Express in Nice today,' she confided like a long-lost sister, sitting at the far end of the bench. 'God us an aerogramme – tell the lady, pa: that purdy little blue thang...'

He quoted a message that evidently came from some commune in Oregon or deepest Nor Cal: '"Now, we knows ya havin' a ball over there, but there's a heap lotta doin' ta be done over here, and Unka Sam points the finger. We want ya. We need ya right here in yer good ol' Amerikin home!"'

The girl crooned a devoted 'Amen!', modulating the first syllable, and all I could think of was Seward with his ridiculous 'Ringadingdings'.

Meanwhile, around in the Senequier, the Englishwoman

was seated on her own. Her Sunbelter had vanished, and she held a hand over her eyes. Just as I was fantasizing her into a high-class Lydia, she lifted it and, looking around, cried:

'Hang about!'

'Madame?' – A waiter efficiently surfaced. 'Quelque chose vous dérange?'

'Yes, but he…' She surged to her feet. 'Harry? I say, Harry?' – fumbling with her bag, 'O that great, horrid American poof! he has the money, you see. I'm afraid I cahn't pay. I –'

The waiter smiled oddly. 'Tu es abandonnée, Madame?'

'Abandonnay? What does that mean? O where has he gone *now*? No I cahn't pay. Really I must get back to…' Calling 'Harry!' and tripping over a table and chairs, she rushed into the night.

The moon passed in and out of racing clouds; boat cables rattled; the town functioned cautiously, cafés half-filled. Cautiously I wandered past them, wondering, half-hoping to find Tony again. But he wasn't in the brightly-lit place when I went by: there were only foreign faces in there now – men grinning, ready to offer you a drink and a ride.

I walked back to the villa. It was five kms and took nearly an hour. The message of the singers kept repeating in my brain in its quaint, up-country tones; and I fantasized that, though we'd grown out of such hippy dreams long before, maybe there was still a vision in it for Tony and me – of making a life in the redwoods or live oaks of Marin, or possibly further north.

Images speeded my pace. Espresso meanwhile was coursing through my blood, agitating it more. The wind was still moaning, the clouds clearing away. The moon and stars peered out brilliant; as I crunched up the drive, I wondered if it was too late to tell him I was sorry and make amends…

'Tony?' I whispered, slipping in the door. 'You here?'

No answer. I touched for his body – nothing in bed.

I watched the underbrush bend under moon-glow. I listened to wind rattle tiles on the roof. Some distance away, a door banged at irregular intervals. And my thoughts raced on, until they were less certain, unconfident, decomposing…

Rain dashed over the roof.

'Lauren?' – A hand shook my body. 'Lauren?'

'Wha'?'

'I have something to tell you.'

'Can't it wait till morning?'

A dream hovered above us, flew past. And the Mistral rushed on on its mission, lashing the spirits of those it had been called down to chase.

5.

The Englishwoman of the Senequier came back in my dreams. She was Lydia now; Seward had long since merged into Alistair and was glowering at the maggoty corpse of a dog while a land-lady rattled on. My Algerian was Rudolf Valentino with a har-don, but as I lay below him he turned into Tony. We started to make love but, before it went far, he was distracted and got up and went out the door to follow some apparition on a breeze.

Then it was Tony, not me, who was twisting in dreams. So I got up and in the grey twilight stood in the door, my nightie blowing back at him like incoming fog.

'Lu-mum,' he murmured.

What was he seeing? her indistinct, suspended in ether, dressed in whitish nothing, a shimmering ideal? But who was this *she*, this otherworldly harpy or muse who animated his nights? Was she young and full like me? pregnant maybe? Was she in the magical time of life or aging, thin-haired, formless, foetus-like, finally reverting to the tomb?

Whoever she was, she was not me, I knew. Probably never had been. Tearing off my nightie, I pulled on a shift. Scribbling a note saying 'Gone to Amex', I set off in a sullen dawn.

At Alistair's apartment, I presented myself to the concierge. After some minutes of waiting, I was invited to go up to the eleventh floor. When the doors of the lift opened, I found myself confronting the latex smile of his ghoul.

'Good afternoon,' Gus crooned like a butler to Vlad the Impaler. 'Mr Moonchild didn't say he was expecting you. They've gone, as it happens. You're welcome to wait if you wish.'

'I was just looking for Seward Barnes.'

The smile squeezed into a grimace, then relaxed into dough. 'Ah. Well, Mr Barnes is at an hotel now. I can get you the name. One moment please.'

He was sucked back into the bowels of the place, leaving me to gaze in a mirror at mottled clouds receding into the harbour.

'Here it is. Hotel Vieux Monaco, onze rue de la Gare. But you are more than welcome to wait here if you'd prefer…'

'I don't have the time, thanks. I'll just try this address.'

'As you please. But Mr Barnes may not be in. I suspect he may've gone off for the day as well.'

I let that float and went away wondering whose fault it was that these folks made you react like a face in an LSD nightmare.

The hotel was not Seward's style. It needed replastering, especially around the art nouveau flounces. Yellow stains dripped down a baby-shit facade; when I opened the door, a large tabby cat flew at me as if chased by a mastiff.

'Mais ma chatte, Ma'm'selle! ma petite bête!' – A plump, huffing dame bumped past in pursuit. 'Tu es très méchante!'

Had everyone lost his beloved in the Mistral?

Her gnarled, be-ringed fingers scooped up the escapee. 'Très méchante!' her voice scolded, 'Tu es très méchante!'

'I'm trying to find a man named Seward Barnes,' I said.

Cat in hand, she went back to her reception-desk. Dropped in an overstuffed armchair, the beast set to using its claws. Exhausted by futile effort, the woman simply shook her hairdo.

'Chambre numéro treize, premier étage. Mais l'escalier est

trop pour une vieille femme. Il faut aller vous-même.'

I thanked her and wound into a skinny stairwell.

'Mais Monsieur est parti depuis quelques heures. Madame est toute seule.' – She made an absurd moue at the feline while saying this, as if trying to tease it out of scorn for anything but its asshole, which it vigorously licked.

'Madame is alone? That's OK.'

'Mais non, Ma'm'selle, attendez...' There were some glasses on a chain which she brought up to her eyes to give me the once-over. 'Vous êtes une amie de – ?'

'I'm a friend, yes.' – Twisting up another turn of the stairs, I showed a resolve not to be stopped.

'Alors, Américains!' you could hear her mutter. 'Où es-tu, méchante? Miaou? Miaou? Très très méchante, où es-tu?'

I should've been ready for the cliché that followed after these preliminaries... The room was dark, the shutters closed over narrow windows at the far end. At first, I imagined that the light, or lack of it, was what made her look so bloody awful; but it was more. Her nose was red; the veins stood out on her temples. Her whole face had gone thinner, sharper, etched with fresh lines. This leanness was accentuated by the fact that she was wrapped in a man's robe way too big for her. Clothing, kleenex, cosmetics et al were of course strewn around: she was in the process of making up but had only gotten halfway there. One hand played with her hair, drawing it back in a knot; the other fidgeted between cigarettes and a bottle of rot-gut. From this, she poured a sip now and then without thinking to offer me one. Maybe she could tell by one of her 'instincts' that I wouldn't've 'fancied' it anyway.

'You're a surprise,' she began, barely batting an eye.

'I came to Nice to check the mail, and just thought I'd just... Tony's not feeling too good, so I thought – ' I knocked over an overfilled ashtray.

'Fuck it,' she breezed as I knelt to clean up. 'Hardly in a state to see anybody this a.m.'

'It's after two.'

'Really? I've just now been sleeping.'

New ciggie in hand, she fumbled in a mess of pink kleenex, apparently in search of a light. Rising, she marched the length of the small space on her platforms, swaying her boyish bum as if to make the point that – whatever else had departed – there was still *that*. Wobbling, she turned back, one hand still playing with the knot of hair. Replunking on bed, she groped in its mess till she came up with a cylindrical lighter. She jetted a flame tall enough to burn off her pencilled-in lashes.

'My new fire… Seward.' – Tossing it aside, she took up a mirror. 'Must look a fright. This hair!'

'What about it?'

'Whot about it? Don't fool me. Why I ever dyed it that dreadful colour…'

'Isn't bad.'

'It's bloody awful on me and you know it. You've nearly said so numerous times; so bloody unnatural. Even Seward's owned up and he never notices such things… part of it bloody red, part black – will you look? What is one to do? let it grow out all mousey? dye it again?… Listen:'

She put a finger to lips and, tiptoeing to the door, lay a side of her head against it. Peering at me with sudden animation, she tensed and, as if switching a light on a bedfull of lice, twisted the handle. – The receptionist jerked in surprise.

'Bunjurr, mahdamm!' Lydia crowed mock-cordially.

''jour, 'dame.' – Grimacing, the bad-tempered old thing dusted her way along the banister, as if that's all she had been lurking there for.

Lydia slammed the door behind her. 'Eavesdropping ever since we arrived…' She fell back on the bed laughing. 'Seward's sussed that she's sussed we aren't really married – that ridiculous bit with the passports, which they still go in for; amazing that anyone should give a toss nowadays – and ours aren't even the same country! Such a bore if we want to have a toot; but we put on quite a show when we fuck, I might say – let her have her little loon then, we do. I'm sure she imagines I'm some rather pricey whore, and Seward my pimp. And you're no doubt in on the game with us.'

She laughed till she choked and started to cough. The cough grew violent; it brought tears to her eyes. I reached out to pat her but, waving my hand away, she took a nip of the booze.

'How'd you end up in this place anyway?' I managed once she'd recovered.

'O dramas – cahn't possibly relate all…' Lighting a new fag, she puffed herself up. 'Suffice it to say that it just wasn't on.'

'It?'

'Seward wanted to go to Italy to lunch – some restaurant they'd been to the other time "in the Rolls". Well: Alistair and Gus said they had business and couldn't, though what this business was… Seward gave them "a hard time" till they made it clear that it wasn't so much couldn't as wouldn't, at which point he suggested Piero drive us. Well: we hadn't got further than the bloody lift before Piero, promising that if Seward would just lend him a hundred he'd fix it all straightaway – with Alistair, that is – and get the bread back by evening, which sounded all right; and, well, you know how lovely and loose Seward is – agreed, and Piero promised to meet back up at some bar by the Casino in an hour, but it must've been four before he turned up, very stoned and totally unable to speak – and of course he has troubles even when straight – and gave us a toot of something that was either the heaviest I've ever had or, Seward reckons… but then sometimes I wonder just how much he knows about these things. Any rate, we went back – Piero utterly stoned, as I say – and straightaway begins screaming at each other in bloody French, and that awful Gus in his Arabic – O, such a purple great drama afoot! Seward says that Piero says that Gus has something to do with some scene or other I don't at all understand – nor approve of, I might add – and it was Gus who actually sussed just how smacked-up he was. I never quite gathered: were they worried or angry? In any case, it was obvious we could not spend one more hour in that; so we started to look for a hotel – whereupon Seward discovered how little bread he had.'

She paused to fret with her various props, and I realized that I'd only been half-listening. The other half of me had reverted to an evening on the patio at the villa – it seemed years ago now – when she'd been holding forth about how 'into petty things like pumm fritts' we were and condemning our 'boringness', particularly Tony's. 'I don't think about meals in London,' she had said; 'I think about what everyone else is doing! but here they're bloody nearly all we've got!'... O she had reigned supreme that balmy night! The sun had just gone down, and she was wearing the silver lamé thing that made her glow in the dark. 'I make an act out of petty things – one must get something from them: humour perhaps, something. Utterly futile to get uptight about them, though one cahn't ignore them entirely; just at the moment they seem to be everything, which must mean they've become extremely important or we extremely trivial, I'm not sure which...' Her good sense had been irrefutable then, even if we'd resented it. Now all was changing. Entropy – or was it male envy? – had been dragging her down.

'But that wasn't the end of it,' she exhaled, having nearly torched her hair trying to jet a new fag. 'He had to get that bread back. That's all there is to get to London on!'

'So what did you do?' I asked after a pause in which she seemed to lose track of where she was or what saying.

'Well: as soon as we got here, he phoned; but Alistair wasn't in, so he talked to Piero and they decided – don't ask me, I was never consulted – that the best thing would be for him to invite him out to dinner and put it to him then; so we ended up taking them – the entire lot – for this outrageous nosh without the least idea of how to pay. And you know, Rose, for some reason I became the target of every innuendo, every cut – and you know how cutting that Alistair can be. As a rule I can handle the type perfectly, but do you know, it was as if I was totally unable to make one intelligent remark? And the worst part was that I had this humiliating feeling that, because of the money... O can't you see how boring and awful? I just sat there and smiled, and took it and took it until – thank the Lord – he became bored and started in on Piero. And then the bill came, and it was poor Seward's turn.'

I didn't worry about her calling me Rose. Perched on that bed, it seemed almost natural for her to confuse herself with the little Napoleona of Parkway. At the same time, this sign of decay brought back another moment on that patio when, after one of her speeches on astrology, I'd asked what she thought happened to people when they died. 'I believe,' she had said, 'that there must be some existence after this, though I can't prove a thing. I know there are facts – when I read books, I come on them – but they're just things I seem to've known all along. Sometimes I wish I could store up all the facts so that when I come against these cynical types who need everything spelt out I could turn them on. But you see I don't need facts, so how can I store them? Yes, I'm certain there's something; not just nothing. I haven't sussed what it is yet, but whatever, I'm certain it's good...' She had been unusually otherworldly then, silhouetted against sunset: even Tony, who argued so bitterly against her 'blind faith', had been temporarily transfixed. Tony, however, was not the male in question in this room. Nor was this Lyddie remotely the creature of his 20th century fox fantasies.

'"Poor Seward"?!' I repeated in a tone she had often used, trying to bring her back from staring into a black hole.

'Yes? O. Well... this morning he got up suddenly and said, "Right: I am going to Alistair's and get that money one way or the other!" – O it was lovely: just the way you Americans *will* be when you've finally made up your minds. I thought of your Tony... So then: he's down there right now.'

'No he isn't. I was just there. That fucking Gus's the only one around.'

She turned. Could you catch a hint of the shakes? Grabbing the lighter, she torched a new fag, though the last one still lay smouldering.

'But I really must get back to London...' she breathed.

'Tony and I can help with that.'

'Tony?' – She looked at me. 'You can't afford it.'

'Hey, he may be tight, but we can spring enough to get you back home on.'

Her look began to revolve again, as if some foreign entity were shaping itself up in the middle distance. It gave me the creeps, so I stood to open the shutters. She put a hand over her eyes, though it was still really pathetically grey out there. Sitting down again at the foot of the bed, I let things drift a minute. Then a perverse instinct took hold of me:

'Lydia, I had something I came here to tell you... I, you – I mean, Tony's had this dream. It was a vision, like recurring – nightmare maybe. He's in bed this morning with fever. He keeps trying to think it isn't you he's seeing, but it was like you calling out to him in the night – I'm sure of it.

'I know this sounds weird, and you wouldn't do it; but I have to get to the truth some way, and he's not going to have the balls to tell me. If it's you he's after, well – I have to see things for what they are now. I'm not going to fight to hang onto a guy who doesn't want me completely, like you say. If he's gotta sew his wild oats and have a fling with what he thinks is this exotic European female, let him. It's not like you were some kind of witch really – you're a human being too, vulnerable like the rest of us; and maybe you need him more than me anyway.

'What happened that day on the beach was that he was scared – I know: I was up in the trees watching. You think maybe he didn't fancy it, but I know what was going on really. He was scared that he couldn't measure up to your standard – also confused maybe because of me, but fuck that. I've made my decision – at least am trying to. Fuck American Express! I came here to tell you that if you want the little shit, you can have him.'

She was gazing at me as if I were speaking through a megaphone on the moon. And I might've asked myself then how much the Mistral had addled my brain too, but sometimes even supposedly prosaic people can prefer trance-life to common sense, can't they?

'O I really must get back to London,' she repeated, as if not having heard a word.

'Fuck London! you have the world at your feet!' – What kind of illusion was I trying to get off on, or project onto, her?

'But what about you, Rose?' – She looked older, sober and hardly cracked.

'This is Lauren,' I corrected. 'And I want to get home too, just like you.'

That seemed to wake her. 'Home, did you say? But he doesn't – is that it? Why doesn't he, then? You two aren't going to split up, are you? But of course, you're not sure. He had a vision, did you say? a nightmare, did you call it?'

'You don't understand...' Was coming unhinged contagious, or was this some zero-sum game between us which meant that, as soon as she began to swing back toward rationality, I was impelled out toward self-destructiveness? 'What I meant was, I think that – he's just beginning to be in love.'

'In love?!' she echoed. 'Isn't that what you said, "in love"?!' She cackled till she choked and was crying again. 'O you sweet little cow – "In love"?! But that is so very, very *beautiful*. And so very, very... Honestly, you must either think I'm a child or – '

'I don't think you're anything but – '

' – you're having me on.'

' – what you are, will you listen? Especially here, in this place you've gotten yourself into... Lyddie, I'm just trying to help. Get you out of this mess and off somewhere where you can... Look, if you want Corsica – if you want – '

'Help *me*?! That's what you want, is it? But what makes you think I need help then? Why is it everyone wants to treat me like a sick child suddenly? I do not want to be a sick child, thank you very much; and I am not looking for some solemn, over-protective boy to try to play daddy for me, so you can put away your "weird" fantasy of trying to pass him on. What daft ego-trip makes you think I would ever've wanted him in the first place?

'O do stop looking at me as if I'm so grey and pathetic! I'm magnificent compared to what you'll be at my age: read the truth in the mirror! You may think I need your kind of thing, but I don't. I want something exciting! someone at least half worth prancing around the world after. A faint heart and limp will never won a fair lady, not even a thirty-five year old one. Nor could it ever begin to bring back a piece of that *sensation* in me!'

*

I've been telling this tale to myself for a decade or more and never get it exactly right. There are details I leave out and some I put in that never happened that way. Am I a born liar, as Tony contended, or is it just that I'm afraid that the entire truth might cloud over the true message?

But what is that 'message'? that good girls and bad women are two sides of one coin? that fat girls become vixens just as easily as foxes, or that a fox can end up being some kind of saint? Is it that women should stop running after pretty boys for once and all? But every half-baked feminist has been saying that for years, and it hasn't made a teaspoon-full of difference.

Maybe the message is that all of us have some private dream of beauty, and death; that we're all in quest of schadenfreude and redemption, even if none of us has much idea of where to find them in this vale of tears. Maybe it has to do with Youth vs Age, or Old World vs New; or maybe Lydia was some hip Mrs Thatcher and her life a prevision of the Fast Lane we would swerve into in the 1980s, with Seward as Ron R. and the land-lady and Arab playing their well-scripted roles.

Whatever the moral, the style reminds me that we didn't come from a time or a place drenched in the narrative graces. We came from a milieu where the visual 'walked tall' and all that inner stuff – the sad stuff of meaning – got treated with ominous awkwardness. So I guess I should just end my story here without more speculating. Its message may best be left between me and my shrink, as Seward says. Or between me and Lyddie, as she might've contended, if she were still around to natter about it.

That image of her withered and alone receded as I drove back down the coast. An image of her intense and indomitable reasserted itself, which may be what she'd intended. The first was unreal, I told myself: only the phantom of some odd bad moment. The second faded into unreality too soon enough: who could believe that that powerful Lyddie was much more than a facade?

Still, what truth can there be if everything is seen to turn into its opposite finally? Why bother caring about human nature if you're always going to conclude it's as fickle as a mistral? What kind of energy can ever be trusted if it's always in ebb and flow, lawless, with no predictable authority to control it – not even the 'entropy' Seward goes on about in his pseudo-scientific post-Einsteinianity?

I didn't think these things through then. I was determined, as Tony accused, to think nothing through with more sophistication than a silly bubble-gum-chewer. Sensual life was everything to me then: the sunset, which faded; the moon, which rose behind a receding corniche and climbed the heavens, crossing until it grew small, more defined, hyper-intense.

Reaching the limit of its power, it settled smack in my path. From across the waters, it beckoned; and as I drove into its laddered silveriness, I gazed at a mythic, cinematic illusion of someone standing on a cliff-top against the light and me merging into *her*, caressed by silky whites, which gathered and spread and yearned toward the horizon, as if on a soft breath of breeze.

Our humble Volkswagen flew out and around her, over the rippling path of her moonshine until – bang! A puncture.

I sat in the wind scared, cross, cursing like Tony in the north of England. Damn these machines that had so much power to impel us back into the nerve-jangling here-and-now!

Working the jack, I got the thing up. Eventually it was drivable on a pathetic excuse of a spare. Incredibly carefully, I carried on, the vehicle seeming to teeter. Or was it me?

By Ste Maxime, the wind had gone wild again. The moon had put her veil on and, by the time I'd reached our villa, fat drops of rain were splatting against the windshield.

Inside, I lay down beside him. Touching his head, I could tell he'd had the sweats but was sleeping them off. Feeling a jab at the base of my belly, I rolled onto my back and listened to the storm wail for her demon lover... She kept at it for hours, holding me off from dreams, leading me down roads through shapely shadows until – when I opened my eyes – it was day.

He was asleep, still. Like a thief in twilight I got up and packed. Drawing my hair back, I wove it into Navaho braids. Scouting around, I made sure that everything was, like, tied up in ribbon. Then I opened his notebook and sat down to write.

His blond, tousled head might have been a five-year-old's as he fought there in sleep. And you can bet there were tears in my eyes too when I finally ripped out the page.

'Do you intend to sleep until midsummer night?' she asked of the same sleepy-head less than ten minutes later.

I'd almost run into her crunching up the drive. At first, eyes still glazed, I hadn't recognized the spectre. Head shorn and body hid under shapeless fatigues; the platform heels, trendy gear and pressed-out bust vanished – she was a child-of-the-road now: a wraith-like mirror-image of me, kicking up stones to get to us. So: what was her game to be *this* time?

With the silent step of a squaw, I slipped back to the far side of the villa and leaned behind the storm-door:

'What the hell've you done?' was his groggy reply. – You could just make them out, striped behind wooden slats, him pulled up on a pillow, her primping that freshly sheared skull.

'I did it last night, after a little bird told me a few home truths. I was going mad in that pathetic little room... Hardly a professional job, as you see: still a bit of red about; have to have that off in London. Quite amazing how it makes one feel, though. I don't know whether it's started the change or whether a change afoot started it. Any rate, I feel absolutely a new woman – and may well become one.'

He was half-grinning; tired, but sweet. It was a picture of naïveté, his uncalculated, hers part-undetected, both youthful and, you might say, all-too-human.

'I think Seward thinks it's wretched,' she joked.

'Well I dig it, Lyddie.'

'Good. Because it does make a difference.'

I felt for her then, and had a new stab in the gut.

'So how come you're here?' he asked.

'Hitchhiked,' she answered, improbably.

'Hitchhiked? all the way from – '

'I told you a change was afoot. O I was nervous as a silly cow – scared to death at one point. Some geezer in a minute rockety thing got me from Nice to St Raphaël in fifteen minutes.'

'But it takes over an hour!'

'But we were on the autoroute, see, and going incredibly fast. I peered over once: two hundred somethings it read. Scared lit'rally to the point of wetting me knickers. But then I realized that, if it must be, it must be, and no doubt is intended to be, and I must just accept and dig it.'

'"It"?'

'Whatever determines it all, obviously.' – Giggling, she went on: 'He was more than your normal frog driver. And despite the fact we were zooming along at that amazing speed, there didn't seem to be the slightest danger. He knew exactly what he was on about; by the time we'd reached St Raphaël, I found I'd begun to find it quite thrilling. Always fancied a bit of speed, actually... The one who picked me up then – O Tony, don't you see? all my nervousness, all my believing the worst in people turns out to've been bloody pointless!'

She slid her hands in the pockets of the baggy trousers she'd put on and spread her legs in a new, as if feminist stance. By then he'd become ready to have her, you could tell – only Lydia, being Lyddie, had to talk the moment away:

'Suffice it to say that Seward came back very late, and very stoned and without the money. I felt so awful: it's so much my fault really. I'm not blaming myself, just trying to... I mean, you must admit – I must admit – that I had some hand in creating this mess. O Tony, I've seen how far I've wandered through it all: from the person I've always wanted to be, worked to be. I've begun to see things; remember… can't you tell what I'm on about?' – She dropped her eyes to the floor. 'Cahn't explain quite yet… shattered actually.'

She leaned down and, when she'd straightened, there was my note in her hand. At some point, probably when she'd opened the door, it had fluttered off his pillow. Now before he could see it, she stuffed it into a trouser pocket.

'I lay awake pondering,' she carried on. 'Seward said he was going back to them in the morning, and gradually it began to dawn on me' – taking her hand from the pocket – 'the principle, you see' – putting it back in – 'how wrong it would be for me to try to stop him.' She took a step toward him… 'Well: very early this morning, being ever so careful with my words so that he wouldn't feel criticized or deserted, I wrote a note saying I was coming to make sure you lot didn't split without us and that I'd wait for him here until he arrived.' She slipped the note from the pocket – 'Should think he'd be here tomorrow at the latest, don't you? You two can wait a day or so longer, no?' – and dropped it back on the floor where she'd found it. 'O Tony, you don't know how grateful I am you sent me that little bird yesterday! You don't know how important it is to me to know I have someone to – turn to.' She herself turned now to the doorway and sighed, 'But I mustn't go on with you just waking like this. Where *is* Lauren, by the way?'

How slyly theatrical she was, to the end! And how angry it made me, even though I'd supposedly given him up.

'I was dead to the world till you came,' is all he could get out. 'What time is it anyway?'

'Eleven-thirty or so.'

'Must have gone into town.'

'Yes?' – She took another step toward him, as if idly, then stooped. 'Hello, what is this?' – Rising with the note in her hand, she uncrumpled it. A look of alarm crossed her features as, gazing up, she held it out.

'"My dear love,"' he read, taking it, '"I'm writing tonight

because I don't know if I'm going to have a chance to see you again before I go and don't want to disturb you while you're still sick. My Algerian friend asked me if I wanted to hitch a ride to Paris with him – "' He set it down.

She took it up: "'Senaqweer in the morning – leaving around noon – don't take this to mean I don't love you very much, but…"' She crumpled it. 'O my God,' she murmured. 'O yes! this is my fault too! I put that bitter idea in her head – that everybody should be on their own… Of course I did, Tony – don't you see? how I argued and bitched; tried to get at you every chance I had? You seemed so untouchable, sort of, and in control. And you two had such a beautiful thing together!'

'Maybe it wasn't so beautiful after all.'

'But it was! don't you see? No one has perfection; that's a great teenage myth, as you'd say: real things take time… You know what she said to me? it was so lovely and thoughtful. She said: "But don't you think two people have a responsibility to try to make it work even if it's not perfect?" – She was so totally right, Tony! And I set about immediately to destroy it!'

He tried to answer, but she threw out a hand:

'No. No more chat! it's nearly midday. If you go right now, you may still be able to catch her.'

'I can't do that.'

'Whot do you mean, "Cahn't do that"? You must do that! Don't you understand: that's exactly what she expects you to do? make some move to show her you love her? love *her* for once and for all, her alone? Haven't you sussed anything about women by now? Lord, the way you just sit there one might think you didn't want her. You *must* go, while you have a chance!'

He moved not a muscle.

Crushing the note in a fist, she declaimed:

'Right then: if you won't, I will! Yes, maybe that would be the proper thing, considering.' – And stuffing it into her pocket a last time, she demanded: 'Where're your keys then?… Well come on, you must have your keys.'

He got up, naked as the day he was born; and right then I

should have realized how far gone he was – or was he? What was *his* game finally as, fumbling in his jeans, he found the keys where I'd put them when I'd come in.

'There's a good lad…' She kissed his forehead as if with no more than maternal interest and, despite his all-too-pretty bod offered up, said, 'Back straightaway.' – Then she was off with a sprite's zest; the Volkswagen revved as if to explode; gears ground, and it was away down the drive.

I don't know how long I stood there. I was in a kind of a daze. Sometimes I think I dreamed the whole thing before it hap-pened. Anyway, the next I knew there was the sound of another car, very smooth, very low, spitting up gravel toward us; then Seward's voice, bathed in inebriate fluid, whanging, 'Wha's hap'ning? Seen Lyddie? Left a note; said ta meet her…'

'She went into town,' Tony answered almost inaudibly. 'I'm surprised you didn't run into her on your way.'

'Didn't run into nothin' but that fuckin' weirdo smack in the road lookin' as if we'd run over 'is prize bitch. Wanna toke?' A suck-suck of hyperventilation… 'Godda be the car, man, Citroën-Maserati, fantastic; all wanna stare at 'em, maybe have ta get outa Rollses after all. Wanna toke?' Sssssskkkkkhhhhh… 'Went inta town, huh? Why? What're you up to this a.m.?'

'Waiting.'

'For what, man? Shit weather, huh?'

'Mistral.'

'No shit? Where's the wind?'

'It comes and it goes.'

'Idn'a mistral then. Mistrals, the wind stays all the time – meteorological fact, all the time. Read about it. Wanna toke?' Wwwooosssfh… 'Inta town, huh? Well, maybe we'll find 'er. Gonna take Alistair an' Piero ta see the most far-out yacht in the world, wanna come? Nothin' ta do in this fuckin' dump, man. You're not gonna go to the beach, are you?'

'I'll stay here.'

''K, be that way; your funeral.'

With that he clumped off and the sound of the car, cool and rich, whished away. There was a vague commotion and bark in the distance. I slipped around the villa and was making my way through the brush by the drive when the ancient farmer appeared out of an oleander and ran up to the patio.

His mouth was gaping, his teeth spittled, his eyes a hell-fire red. 'Venez!' he commanded. 'Venez! Venez!' – Grabbing Tony by a wrist, 'Là-bas! Venez, là-bas!'

What foolish thing had Seward and Co run down in their smooth whir? a chicken? dog? Had the farmhouse been hit? – The old guy gave no hint; he just led Tony away headlong, jerking him by a belt-loop of the jeans I'd mended.

Following them, I called out. Looking back, he saw me, but by the time the farmer had led him to the place, I was the last thing he was going to worry about.

Ruts made by the car had veered off the track just where it turned at the farmhouse. An olive tree, freshly wounded, was bent over on its side.

'J'vais à la gendarmerie!' the man muttered and, releasing him, hurried away.

Peering over a shale wall into the vineyard below, you could see at the bottom of a short drop the Volkswagen. It was bashed in the front and upturned on its roof. Directly underneath it was a bundle of blanket.

I felt sick.

He leapt down.

Her tiny head, shorn, was cut in two places, neither apparently serious. There was some blood at her hairline and over her eyes, which were shut. They opened when she heard him kneel down beside her.

'Just a bit of shock, I should think. Daft… Get me a ciggie?'

I stood above staring as he fished the pack from her pocket and lit one like they used to in old movies.

'Bloody fool to rush off like that…'

'I always hated that machine anyway,' he observed of the wreck, into whose pinging inertia he flicked the burnt match.

The left fender was crushed, the windshield spider-webbed, the roof accordioned like a corrugated trash-can.

'You smoke this,' she managed. 'Doesn't taste nice.'

'Lie still.'

'A few scrapes from the windscreen and a horrible pain in the gut, which I put down to shock... but I did take an awful jolt. Thank God it wasn't in the tit.' – She chuckled.

He half-grinned.

'Must look bloody awful... Good job I chopped my hair: no doubt they'll want to shave the rest. Daft... Gone for help, has he? He was lovely, that bloke. Pulled me from the car, and – O!'

'Don't talk.'

'I was all crumpled up between the wheel and... Yes, it does hurt some. You don't suppose – '

'I suppose nothing till we get a doctor.'

She shut her eyes and lay still, a shorn child who's taken a fall. 'Don't be daft. You must go find Lauren while – '

'I'll get to her soon enough.'

Twisting with difficulty, she fished the note from her pocket. 'It was my fault, Tony. I have to confess – ' A blast of wind rushed in to blow it out of her hand. 'What was that?'

'Only the wind.'

'It's lovely. But so cold.'

'Are you cold?'

'I'd've been frigid if he hadn't wrapped me. He was very kind... I wish Seward were – O!'

'Don't talk.'

'But Dion, I must tell you. Do you know, I think something's started between Seward and me?'

'Shuddup an' lay still.'

She giggled. 'Yes, Daddy.'

Now the wind rushed in again and this time kept coming. Clouds raced across the sky in a phalanx of grey.

'But it's so cold – I can't bear it.'

He motioned to me, 'Get more blankets.'

'No, don't leave!'

'I'm not leaving,' he said and motioned again, but how could I unfreeze myself from where I lurked?

'Put your arms around me?'

So he lay out next to her and slipped one arm under the blanket and the other over her chest, spooning his body around her like he had with me so many times…

'Thank you. You're good, Tony; I'm so sorry. It was that –'

'Don't speak.'

' – dog, big black dog. I tried to miss him, but – O! daft. My heart's beating like a ruddy –'

'Sssssssh! I can feel. Don't.' – He moved his hand down to stroke around the slim waist; tears were hot in my sockets.

'Pain's so useless,' she went on. 'I don't want to live with pain; I want to be happy. I want to be good now: simple, like Lauren. I want –'

'Shut up.'

'It's so cold, on my head. Can't you do something?'

He moved his free hand up and over her wound.

'No!… hurts.'

'Sorry.'

'Perhaps –' She agitated the blanket.

'Over your head?'

'Um.'

'But you won't be able to breathe.'

'Don't be daft.'

He looked to me for a moment – was it for consent?!

'All right,' he muttered, as if decided. 'But I'm going to grunt every fifteen seconds. And if you don't grunt back immediately, it comes off.'

She giggled. 'Whatever you say – Daddy.'

So he pulled the blanket up over and after fifteen seconds grunted gently.

'Daddy does have a sense of humour after all,' she breathed.

After another fifteen seconds, he grunted.

A giggle came up: 'Yes.'

After another fifteen, the answer was fainter:

'Uh-huh.'
Then much fainter:
'Umm.'
Until there was no response.
'Lydia,' he whispered. 'Lydia?'
We waited.
'Lyddie?'

***

— St Tropez, Paris, 1973

ISOLA BELLA

The whole place, in its huge elegance, the grace of its conception and the beauty of its detail, was more than ever like a great drawing-room, the drawing-room of Europe, profaned and bewildered by some reverse of fortune.

– Henry James

He had acquired the power to live in the imagination. It was a fatal capacity. He had at one time lived wildly, at other times in retreat. Now he lived almost all possibilities in advance in the mind. Progressively he wondered if the moment had come when he no longer lived anything actually.

This was the 'inward romantic principle' of middle age, he surmised, turning back from the lagoon. It was a condition of bliss of a kind – also perhaps symptom of senescence? A life lived in the mind lives off the mind, does it not? A constant eating away of mind by mind may begin as the polite filling of a plate at a feast but end as a ravenous foraging at dust-bins, no?

Where on earth had such baroque similes come from, he mused, admiring a swath of palazzi. Would growing old detach him more and more into Jamesian phantasms? What lagoon of the spirit did such imagery burble up from? Or was it simply a matter of what one ate? or of sexual continence? The illustrious Master had become a capon: plump, sublimated, pate balding, face rounding, figure not fat precisely nor fleshly but puffed out like a bird to be made into foie gras. Is that what he too would become, or should? If so, how would metamorphosis occur? devotion to appetites other than the full physical? – One loved food, one drank wine, and both better when of fine quality. Carine's wealth had allowed it: a feasting on ortolans, as it were. (This was figurative: Anthony Thomas, Ph.D., despite occasional pomp, was not sure what the word really meant.)

Dear Carine... He envisaged her walking across the piazza to meet him before he had even selected a seat, half against his sense of taste, at Florian's. It was three-quarters of an hour before she was meant to appear, yet he saw her already as she had been one evening in Knightsbridge after a long day of work and not being able to find a cab. He had been coming from Sloane Square, she from the Brompton Road; and as he had watched her grow large by the Scottish church, hair blown back at the temples on account of her rush, eyes gazing upwards as if a baby's not quite used to habits of sight, he had loved her, surely, very much. Theirs had been a long, certain, steady kind of loving, weathered over ten years, having survived heat and frost because the weather inside had been sweet, their souls being the right souls whatever an outer world might have hurled at them. He had known her through one life-threatening disease; she had sometimes claimed that it was he that enabled her to recover but, uneasy with compliment, he had shrugged it off, knowing that in some ways he had been the one who had led her to death's door in the first place. – Or was this too fanciful? Is any individual ever truly responsible for what happens to another, in body, or soul? If so, he was of course responsible also for the way in which she had transformed through the years into the shape walking quick-stepped past St Andrew's Kirk. And was it at that moment that he had possibly first noted (he'd had inklings before but never seen clearly) that something profound had altered in her? that, having reached a certain age and degree in attainment, a subtle genetic balance had tipped and something *other* become dominant? Always in youth, she had summed up a kind of Mendelssohnic Jewishness for him: light as gossamer, Giselle-like, balletic – as if some Sephardi enchantress, mignonne, delicate as a sprite out of some Arabian Night. But there against the grey stone, as her heels had tapped the trottoir into Lennox Gardens, he could see more and more what had transformed her into a sure businesswoman – a bulk and toughness vs the odds that didn't so much belie her grace as make counterpoint to it; reinforced it with solidity. This too he admired, though perhaps it evoked less of the protective spirit of the superior male. It didn't make him feel inferior quite either, only slightly more *other* than he had once been: a fraction more on the outside; not, on some level, quite as necessary. And yet as he thought this, a second thought pressed in; because, if her ankles had thickened and jawline expanded, if her designer suits made her appear somehow invulnerable, still you could glimpse just how precarious her existence had become inwardly. She was no longer the overtly frangible child that patronizing male egos could preen themselves over, spreading their wings as if mother birds – though with more than a little of the vain insouciance of peacocks. She seemed to daunt men subtly now. Hadn't he noticed them whispering sometimes, seeing or half-perceiving that his lot as sexual being must be nearly over because he had wedded himself to this beyond-purely-feminine embodiment? this triumphant business-woman whose feet splayed slightly as she approached, whose eyes behind glasses seemed to half-squint to discern him, whose arms and hips defied the cut of her fashion to appear a touch akimbo, gawky, belonging to a schoolgirl whose parent had gently mocked her (out of jealousy? caring?) for having the build of an uncoordinated tomboy?

O the pathos! O the small cruelties and infinitesimal slights by which a beloved is pricked, which make us love her the more! So Anthony Thomas ejaculated in mind as he settled on an ersatz wicker chair and prepared to wait by re-adjusting himself to the literary-cinematic cliché of the setting…

He couldn't, of course, tell Carine how his thoughts ran. She would feel he was patronizing, and in his condition as half-de facto kept man this was an illusion he could ill afford. He couldn't, above all, tell her what was entering his life back in London, threatening to flood it, like the lagoon lapping the edges of this most serene construction out of the sea. He longed to confide in her. He felt that on some interior level she *knew* – women do, as they say; and dear Carine, for all her transcendence of mundane witchery, had antennae like the rest. He would have known, after all, had something equivalent been happening in her. Indeed at times he had even suspected that, on some level, her spirit had wandered: that in some etheric emanation she may have been made love to by some colleague or other in her property empire. Or no, that was inexact. The truth was that she was pure – far purer than he in this imaginative aspect; driven less by the four horses of Eros, so that faithlessness, if she had ever indulged in it, would have been directed at the one, not the many. A roving eye seeking salvation in every fine face – or in his case, aesthetic fulfilment – was not her vice. If she'd had a vice, it would have been sentiment. And it was a sentimental attachment that had seemed now and then to have drawn her from him: a married man she adored, who, though wildly attractive in her eyes, he was sure, had been made years before into an emotional safe haven by virtue not only of being unavailable but also of some inexact flaw in his nature – some obscure Celtic downdraught that had limited his trajectory in their profession and left his body prey to the unsympathetic twinges of a 'bad back'. No, her love for *this* other – let's call him Edmund – had never been 'real', Tony reassured himself. There had been a phase, and not so unrecent, when he had fretted as she'd come home late over whether he, Edmund, might have convinced her to go with him one day, once his children were grown and wife had fled on the wings of her obvious desire for something more sensational. She, Edmund's wife, was a blonde and Celt too – but did such categories matter? Tony Thomas now shifted in brooding to Jung and notions from first half of the 20th century, to wit: that elements deep in our genes and traditions, features of being that have nothing visible to do with our environment, become more motivating as we grow old. But he left off this topic almost as soon as it came to him, the moral doctrine of his career having blocked such reflections, the ethno-racial terms being verboten – or at least not 'politically correct' – as in academic life he'd had

constantly to learn. One could only stray so far from civilization's dominant, if temporal, party-line…

But *she* was a Celt too, he reflected – a Celt to her soul, this
angel or demon who'd been threatening their serenity. 'The
Celt is the disintegrative element,' D. H. Lawrence had written
of European civilization in his day, and so would it prove now
in Tony's life? But what was a 'Celt' anyway – some wild spirit
with hair in the wind and songs of yore in her teeth? He had
known some before. Carine had too. She'd been in love with a
Welsh artist prior to meeting him – that liaison had indeed been
the making and almost breaking of their precipitate marriage.
And what had this rival, Oliver Murrie or Merrie, been about?
Could some characteristic in *him* have explained the yearning
that came on Tony now, like an infectious disease? – He tried to
distinguish some face or feature in the crowd that might bring
their old friend back. What had summed him up? reddish hair,
rounded face, turned-up nose, violet eyes? *She* had them all
equally. But then, Oliver's body had thickened in early middle
age, hadn't it? whereas hers seemed as if made out of ether and
twigs; out of branches twisted up in some dense forest pas de
deux; out of elves and white witches draped in Hibernian moss;
out of sad-eyed damosels of the lowlands. Wasn't she in fact his
'belle dame sans merci'? Hadn't he, after all, in this age of pru-
dence – his good marriage – still not grown wise enough to be
proof against that Dead Poets' Society sort of thing?

O Shakespeare! O you British and Irish and English! how
much deracination you've caused through your ancient,
unburied cults! your creatures of romance! – He thought of
Berlioz and how he'd lit up with fire; of his *Symphonie fantas-
tique* and other inspirations produced in the blaze experienced
watching Harriet Smithson play Ophelia and Juliet. Though
he'd hardly understood a word of English, he'd hurled himself
off in her slipstream, into an enchantment as extreme and futile
as Titiana's for Bottom. Only it had not ended in bathos and
laughter for him. Grief, grief, grief, it had come to, and no great
creativity after that initial surge, and even less following her long

illness and death... But what music! Could anything move him more at his stage, Tony mused, than the trio from *Beatrice et Bénédict* or the overture from *Roméo et Juliette*? And wasn't that something? Wasn't it in fact close to everything?

His mind shifted. What would she be doing at this exact time? Was the spell she had cast – a spell in reflection of what she had claimed he'd evoked out of her – becoming a memory she was now getting over? 'The time will be different next week,' she'd commented when he'd said he had to go away. And what had that meant? that she was afraid he might change? that the enchantment cast by her elfin self might wear off? But what did she know about *his* type of spirit? Had she read Stendhal? Could she recognize how the power of time and space, of even one week and less than a thousand miles, might evoke crystallization? And if she did not, did it mean that she herself had no sense of absence making the heart grow fonder? that she could only believe in her impulses if they were met instantly in an expected way? that if a man hesitated, it could only denote that she'd been wrong in the first place? that she'd cast her net after an inappropriate prey? And wouldn't that suggest in the end, or even after a short apartness, that *she* would be liable to alter course? that having got no guarantee or down-payment, as it were, she would lapse on these scores despite all her protestation that he should place faith in her?

Tony wound himself round entertaining these fears, though feeling at the same time how life might become easier on the instant if they were to prove valid. He'd be back where he'd started: back with Carine in their admirable marriage; back in his solid, middle-aged habits of love – of love as affection and sibling-like knowledge, plus a certain deadness in other respects. And that was the real issue here, wasn't it? a certain deadness, certain death, certainty of death, which made it harder as the years wore on to trouble out just how to live...

A restless night. Morning less than blue, a scent of Venice's corruption. Two or three of the great buildings in the square were covered for renovation. The tourists, as usual, swarmed

– so many more Japanese than when he'd been young; so many more young now, he being old, or oldish… He had come first at twenty, in his first year in Europe. All the dazzlement had ravished his American soul, albeit in a macho way. He'd drunk whisky at Harry's to honour Hemingway; sipped wine with a poet who'd offered to introduce him to the 84-year-old Pound. He had been 'in love' then too doubtless – some Yankee precursor of the posh blondes who would later rain light and torment on his London career, in the era before a young man had grown canny about chances or the character of a good woman. One friend on that visit had thrown his wallet in the air in front of the duomo, to prove to a prostitute that he was able to pay. Another had been pushed into the canal by some revellers when trying to recite by lamplight from a volume the impecunious poet had pressed on them. He himself had led a small rebellion in the university group they had come with, which on return had led in some circular way to his first fully-consummated sexual escapade – that is, outside of the Moonlight Ranch. Dusty days now, gilded in memory… many friends gone: the wallet-tosser a military-industrial pirate, the canal-pushee bankrupted because of an upper-middle-class WASP wife. Tony himself – well, what had *he* turned into? a mere witness? Others had lived more, surely: others like him even, having started out in some privileged suburb. One or two had even felt Europe as he had, or been drawn in (drawn down?) by 'literature': Landon Hurst, anti-Semite, who'd detonated himself; John DuRocher, who'd 'beaten out his exile' like a decent chap, though at what cost? Tony had survived well in general estimation: the 'good' marriage to a half-and-half, Carine being German and Jewish both; the equivocal profession, academic writing, lecturing; an acceptable balance between old world and new, an access of 'civilization'. What was missing now he seemed to have had on the way: passion. Everyone who knew or had known him would recall one or two scarlet times in hippy days, before all this half-subtle scaling of ladders. One or two fantasists – he himself too for years – had even imagined that in some ten or twelve-year-old they could spy evidence of his having fathered a child...

He had just arrived at this crucial point in his reveries when he grew aware for a first time of wanting someone to talk to. The thought was provisional: so jealous was he of the interior journey once commenced that he had argued with Carine in the night. It had been one of those terrible fractions half set off by fatigue which end in recriminations stemming back years – to before the parties had met perhaps. Absence of a father, lack of a mother's breast, irresolvable rivalry with some long-estranged sibling – a great knot of infantile or prenatal 'syndromes' got caught up in these affairs of rhetoric, until they exhausted themselves in repetition, absurdity and among lovers love-making... It had been the first time with her in weeks. Pent-up desire and frustration re the other had driven him entirely off sex with her. But then rage and sorrow over their star-crossed affections had made him, half against his will, stroke and embrace her quite tenderly. And when, afterwards, she had remarked on the state of the sheets and cleaned herself up, it had seemed in his current mood a bad portent, though at some other time he might have been as reluctant as her to lie in the wet place. But something had seemed wrong then, something sad, and not least because the quantity of his emission had had so little to do with where it was directed, though it had at their outset and often through the years. Now it had only signified deferred desire and biological excitement for this *other*: this demon, who had told him over the phone the night before he'd left,

'I want you to be the father of my baby.'

Was it any wonder that Carine had woken up fretful and he so restless that he'd had to crawl off to sleep in the bath?

The faucet had dripped. A generator had rumbled beneath the floor. The 'best hotel in Venice' had kept him awake until dawn... Was it any wonder that he felt haunted now?

Doubtless this was causing his apprehension that someone was watching him. Nor was it just paranoia, or self-importance, though by this stage he was contemplating his life with such intensity that – had he believed in magic or some mode of psychic transmission – he might have imagined himself capable of conjuring forms out of thin air: other selves to confront him, genies, alter egos, even some Mephistopheles to mock and draw him out onto 'another plane'. In truth, hereabouts there were only tourists – not a fact he could complain of, seeing as how he was one too, though it remained slightly off-putting. At least in the aggregate, troops of Japanese weren't inspiring. Nor were his countrymen, waddling big-bummed over the piazza with their inconceivably-shaped wives. The Brits here were far from sylvan emanations: caught on package-holiday, the males seemed by some code to take no cognisance of costume except to make sure it was invisible, while the women wore frocks draped like tents over bodies which for some reason had lost all trace of feminine curve. Why? a diet of white bread, synthetic 'choccie', milky cups of tea? It was a mystery to him how working- and even middle-class mothers of that isle could begin as heart-breakers like his elf and end up like this. But these were generalizations. Towards individual beings, he found it hard to be unkind. One Japanese lady nearby had had a stroke, and the solicitude of her son for her made a poignant tableau, reminding him of mothers, fathers and grandparents whose declines he'd grieved over. And the French ladies at the table adjacent may have been aging, bored, tired and useless to the hot mind of some young Raskalnikov, but who could truly despise them? There was a rigueur there, a thing he had loved in the French all his life: in their language, their confidence, their sure sense of place in this world. And these Americans joking, 'Just one more for the road!' – how could you begrudge them their jollity? Or the Germans, who in manner and appreciation nowadays often seemed the best Europeans?

No, he could not despise mankind, tacky though it made San Marco... 'All these ghastly pigeons,' someone in his ear meanwhile breathed. 'How can you bear to sit here? Why not come to the Accademmia with me? This place is surely too obvious for a chap of your taste.'

The voice had breeding – he could not register it instantly. The hair, he saw, turning, had gone grey at the temples. Apparently undyed, it looked more boyish than he recalled, while the cut of the t-shirt down the gap of her breasts held a suggestivity that she would not have dared in her younger, blue-stockinged days.

Geraldine Scott, whom he now recognized, was another face of the Brit. Neither elf nor tent-lady, she embodied, or once had, the archness and bien-pensant quality of an Oxbridge femme savante, which she was in fact, or had been – one of the coming of her generation – before something had happened. What was it? he could hardly remember. But this transformation... she looked gaunt, more alive, yet desperate, one might conclude. Her clothing was layered: a medley of waistcoat, skirt and shawl down to leather sandals on inelegant feet. Some release of the life-force was implied here. Following it, he recalled the drift of academic chatter – that the woman who had once been appointed youngest female professor in Britain had come to be viewed as 'unsound' and ended by having no job at all. Geraldine belonged to that rare, refined breed: the defrocked academic. Nietzsche, Timothy Leary, Germaine Greer – maybe even that errant countryman of his who had expired here, Mr Pound. But Geraldine... what did he know of her now, he wondered in the space of seconds it took for the smile to fade on her cracked, though still quite full lips.

The face looked away. A hand unnecessarily pushed back at cropped hair... Her first book had been innocuous – a Jane Austen to Virginia Woolf, woman's lit sort of 'study' typical of the mid-'70s: requisite nods to Julia Kristeva, feminism and so on. Somewhat later he'd heard that she'd tried her hand at 'a fiction' – some post-modernist *play* again typical of the era (by now early '80s) with a Kundera-esque Central European setting, though in her case (she'd only been east once on a week-long British Council tour) more imagined than real or journalistic. Tony had not joined the critics in their scepticism: an extract he'd read seemed to him at least as credible as the 'game' *Plütz* being pushed at the time. But then – it must have been around

1989 or '90 with the Wall coming down – something had happened. What?

'Are you waiting for someone?'

'Geraldine! How lovely. Yes, as it happens, I was.'

'Who? Me?'

A flash of jealousy surged – could she detect it fleeing across his forehead? the inner thought, distant dream, beloved elf diving for cover in folds of his brain...

'I wish I could say so. No, in fact it's Carine.'

'Carine? Do I know her?'

'I'm not sure. Have you met my wife?'

'Your wife? Dear man, your face always seemed so open at the conferences we met at. I never suspected you of having become trapped.'

It was mildly insulting; but the right woman could get away with it, so long as the slap was conferred with an appropriate flick of flirtation, as this was.

Geraldine sat. 'If I can't take you to San Stefano, the least I can do is not desert you to enduring this tackiness on your own until your minder shows up.'

The change, if change it was (and he realized now that he had never known her as more than an acquaintance), was that in younger days the academic star had been continent in personality – i.e., whatever the range of her vista as auteur-lecteur, she would never have dared such a grand dame sortie into a colleague's private life. Of course it was a trope, a Lady Bracknellism, a kind of de haut en bas cuteness meant to invite chummery, conspiracy, communion within an élite; undeclared yet implicit we-know-best-ism. Also implied was that – as an American, albeit of 'the best kind' (i.e., expat) – he ought to be flattered to be invited into such intimacy with a True Brit; though on second take, as uncouth as this one now appeared, might it not be the prelude to solicitation for a loan?

'Don't look alarmed, dear. I promise to vanish before she comes, if you can't risk being seen with another woman.'

The jealous elf pinched. Yet oddly, he was pleased. By some

weird alchemy, at least of mind, this challenge made her his.

'Carine doesn't do jealousy,' he stated.

'Are you sure? I can't believe a man of your type doesn't give fair cause.'

How outrageous, the elf protested, coiling deeper into his pate, pillowing herself in spongy matter to watch this would-be rival's performance.

'Anyhow, must be off,' Geraldine sighed. 'Agnieszka... promised to collect her in half an hour.'

At first, Tony thought – or his inner sprite mused for him – that the drift had been more dramatic than foreseen: that in her fall from academia's grace, this woman had landed in the sodality of Natalie Barney, Djuna Barnes etc.; and why not? Wasn't the feminine 'left hand way' part of the great rebellion of literary bohèmes? a legacy of Anglo-Saxon expatriations to various left banks of the 1920s and after? But, there was something else here. A ripple of sorrow accordioned her brow as, looking down, eyes settled on a pair of pigeons. A female, old, soiled, tatty in feather, half-winged, was being pursued by a sheeny cock with breast thrust out lustily.

'Isn't it surprising? You'd think he'd let her alone in the state she's in. Does biology just go on and on?'

At this point Tony recalled. The story went thus: she, Geraldine, had met a young student, male, at a conference outside of Kraków; they had had a fling and, when she had come back to London, it was to discontent – so that shortly, to the gossips' shock, she had quit her job at University College. Where had she fled to then? He hadn't heard. But she was going to tell him now, wasn't she?

'Who's Agnieszka?'

'Did you not know? My daughter.'

'Daughter?'

'It's been how long since you've seen me? Seven years?'

'Possibly.' – He thought. 'Actually, it may be eight.'

'There, you see. Agnieszka's seven... No, don't look shocked – you're not Daddy.'

'I should think not. We never... did we?'

'More's the pity.'

Ugh, his elf said. But in a moment, like the pigeons, the flutter of false levity passed.

'Get me a coffee,' Geraldine sighed, 'and I'll tell you what happened – at least what I'm doing here. Eight years... I guess that must mean you haven't read my Venice book either?'

'Your "Venice book"?'

'You could call it my "Venus book", as it's all about sex. It was through it, or what caused it, that I realized why I couldn't be an academic any more. It first came to me at about the time as what happened – 1991 or '90, I can't quite recall; any rate, the moment of the great change. I don't know now whether the book caused the change or the change it. I hadn't written a thing but articles or reviews for years – which, as you know in our profession is both common and the kiss of death. Unlike some others, I was not prepared to steal my students' ideas, or even those of younger colleagues. I was weary beyond belief of "deconstruction of text" and the usual paraphernalia that absolutely murder fine minds, though I hadn't quite admitted it to myself. When I met Krzysztof, the earth shook. I ran back to London in thorough fear. That's when the book began, *The Counterlife in Venice*. You must've heard of it; came out in '93 – a succès de scandal. If I'd imagined I could turn back to my job until then, the hoohah of the reviews – even tabloid, unheard of for a book like that – disabused me.'

Tony somehow had missed this. Had he been away in the States then?

'I made love to them all,' Geraldine continued. 'I entered their bedrooms, undressed them, fondled their parts large and small, attended to their bowels.'

Was this madness, the elf asked. Who was the woman going on about?

'All the renegades, darling, from Byron to Pound. All the journeymen in Venice who made love to the Muse here: Bob Browning, Art Symons, Dickie Wagner, Tolstoy, Mann... a difficult case, though less so than Proust, whose Serenissima was entirely a Ruskin-based fantasy. I fucked them all silly and then told the tale.'

The elf settled. Here was a nut-case; there was no threat.

Tony Thomas replied: 'How amusing. I'm not sure I quite understand.'

'I mean, instead of an academic study, I found out what created "Beppo", *Tod in Venedig* and so on by imaginary love-affairs with each creator – each at his precious, vulnerable moment of penetration with, or possibly interpenetration by, the Muse.'

'How novel.'

'So the reviewers said, in a word. But academia wasn't having it.'

'I suppose not.'

'Nor the American fat-biography industry.'

'Too unofficial?'

'Too lively.'

'Of course.'

And so: she was not mad, not exactly. Just inspired.

'Anyhow, that's why we're in Venice,' she concluded.

'"We"?'

'Agnieszka and I. She's come with her babsia. The Italian government – at least Commune of Venice – has appreciated my eccentricity. The book sells the city; academically sound or not, it waves the flag of the Wingèd Lion, though that hardly entered my original intention. It's been translated into Italian and several other languages; as a result, I've been selected to be on the panel of judges of an annual literary prize here.'

The elf could snooze now: literary festivals were out of her league. The nap would be brief, though. Once coffee came, Geraldine sighed and began to explain about Agnieszka, and the tone grew less superficial.

She told about her affair with the Polish student:

'Tried to get him to London. He said that like Chopin he didn't have stamina for sophisticated dinners every night and, though that wasn't true – either that he was so weak or I so posh

– I knew what he meant. But we had nowhere else to go. I took leave from UC and went back to Poland with him; he was still living with his mum as they all do till their mid-twenties. If I'd been a man and he a Polish young lady, she might have turned a blind eye in the hopes of a good marriage; but the fact of me being a much older woman made the whole arrangement seem illicit to her. So we took off for the Tatras – mountains so high that the locals talk about chatting with God, or is it the gods? my Polish was never quite up to much: fiendishly difficult language. Of course one got pregnant. The fact was, I had been since nearly the first time we'd gone to bed, but I couldn't've told him – hadn't told him before coming back from London, knowing instinctively that if I did he would run. When I finally got courage, at least three months gone, the reaction was predictable. Like his father before him, the poor boy got drunk. It was not satisfactory, but there we are. He said I'd brought on disaster, not meaning the child only – there were other things my presence in Poland seemed to have caused, or at least coincided with. It was a bad time then, the early '90s, post-Communist recession at its worst, mafias of one kind or another setting up. Krzysztof feared he was under suspicion – something to do with me; I was never quite clear, though at one point when I first got there, I myself had had to deal with an incident so odd and potentially violent that I don't like to think of it now, or admit that it happened… Anyhow, there we were in the high mountains. I told him about the child, and before we'd practically got back down to the Mazowian plain he was off. To Ukraine he's gone. A Sicilian operating in Warsaw owns pizza parlours in Lwów and Kiev: Krzysztof, I'm told, works for him. Don't ask what he does. He appears now and then in the wide-cut Eastern suits they wear. Hard to believe that this "biznezman" was once a student of philology so shy and tongue-tied that I had to coax him to speak, let alone make advances. But there we are. He's "become a man" – i.e., a stranger. Agnieszka, my lovely, sees him sometimes when she stays at her babsia's. His mother is hardly going to let her only grandchild out of sight for long, whatever urge he feels to deny me.'

She fell into silence.

A pain in his spirit indicated the elf was wide-eyed and making motions now in this female's favour. A child at least had been gained – what *she* could give him – though at what cost?

'So, are you happy? Tell me about Agnieszka?'

Geraldine drained her espresso. Her face looked proud, worn. 'We've won through,' came the answer. 'Excruciating at times, of course. For some reason I couldn't go back to England after that, not permanently. Found myself gravitating to Warsaw. The British Studies Institute was eager to offer as much teaching as I liked; gave me a flat too – ghastly by English standards but "luxury" for Poles. Agnieszka grew up quite strong – and beautiful, I'm glad to say. The first years were a madness: I don't know how I coped – friends, colleagues at the institutes around Poland partly; then too this Venice book. No doubt there was also something fully beyond what one could predict or quite understand.'

'You mean?'

'Only that. Something beyond what one could normally comprehend.'

The pigeons and tourists, wingèd lions and horses above the cathedral offered no gloss. Or did they?

'You mean – ?' Tony Thomas started again.

'Nothing I can put a word to,' she concluded. 'I'm no Christian, thank God; and Poland has taught me to have as much faith in the old atheists as anyone else. But… destiny? Hope?'

A full silence now.

By some caprice, he thought back to the grave of Ezra Pound. They had gone there the day before, Carine and he. He had dragged her across town, it being her 'free' day – i.e., sans business meetings. They had started by watching a wedding at San Zaccaria, then walked along the canal called San Lorzeno del Greco, then on to the square dominated by an equestrian statue of Don Colleone. And there at the edge of the waters he had sat weary, blood-sugar low, the demands of the elf on his spirit just then so great that he almost let go of ten years of the sweetest relationship he had ever had. 'How can you say you want to leave me here?' she had asked; 'I brought you to Venice; this is my free day; I don't want you to leave me; I want to see things!' She had stood there above him where he'd slumped by a mooring; and as he'd gazed at her ankles, plump now with the years, he had wondered how this child whose photo he'd adored on his shelf – a six-year-old laughing at daddy because she'd fallen off her trike – could have grown into this grand lady who alone of her sex was invited to conclaves of international property tycoons and listened to because, though shy and cute-as-a-button with him, she provided some delphic presence for them in their world of competing male egos: some female authority figure they needed to rein in their ambition, resolve their plans and get on. This great, simple spirit whom they could admire and feel unthreatened by had stood above him with tears in her eyes – tears he had created – until at last, his fit passing, he had re-arisen, free enough of his elf to put an arm around her and lead them past the Ospedale, down to the embankment where the boats left for San Michele. There they had lingered for lunch – a quarter-flask of wine, simple pasta, due espresse – and she had grown happy to join him on his small pilgrimage. And after the crossing, they had strolled side by side through the stones, a warm breeze wafting beneath cypresses, into the 'Lutheran' enclave where many ancestors rested: old Yankees, Huguenots and at last in the centre errant Ezra himself, whom this woman seated at his table now had, among others, made imaginative love to. Beside Pound under a freshly-inscribed stone had lain the remains of his 101-year-old mistress, interred only a month before, the two to sleep on in permanent expatriate state on this isle, beside the defunctive civilization's most generative sea... On then they had walked, past Diaghilev's tomb, from whose stone a pair of rotting ballet-slippers dangled; then back to the 'mainland' and Ghetto Nuovo, which Carine had not liked. The austere buildings, higher than any others in Venice – did they remind her of a Europe where she'd never been, having, despite property bonanzas in Prague and Budapest, a Western

Jew's healthy phobia of scenes of devastation? The plaques on the wall of the round common space had chilled her, etched as they were with images of 'remembrance': figures like her own crowded into cattle-cars by armed men wearing phallic helmets. Quickly then, they had passed on, towards the Canale Grande, and found a vaporetto to take them back along the outer rim of the city, setting them down under a beatific sun on the Zattare allo Spirito Santo. There they'd drunk Campari along with normal denizens of the place, neither mad nor rich nor oppressed, looking out over to the Guidecca; and her spirits had risen as they always did when she was seated in the waning light with a drink. The dimples had come back into her cheeks; the slight gilt in her hair had glistened as they'd strolled on further towards the Dogana, inspecting pensiones which they promised to return to on some less imposing trip. He had complained of the huge-monied atmosphere of the Danieli where they were staying and of the Cipriani where she had to go for the evening's meal; meanwhile, cutting across the spit of the Dorsoduro along an inner canal still warmed by hours of afternoon sun, they had found a mood like on a day at the seaside prevailing, as if from earliest childhood, perhaps even pre-speech. Passing signs to the Guggenheim, they'd pledged to see it before leaving, though in afterthought he'd remarked, 'Why would I want to see something so essentially American here?' applying a standard incongruous to the one he had put to Pound's grave, though not, as it happened, to Harry's Bar, which Carine would've liked to have gone into once they'd stepped off the traghetto, despite the crowd and a necessity of staying sober for her evening's travail. But he'd kept her on the straight-and-narrow.

'I don't want to go,' she had pouted back at the hotel. 'I don't want to leave you alone for the evening.'

'I'll be OK,' he'd answered. 'I'll find that restaurant you were interested in by La Fenice – check it out.'

And so he had. And it had rained. And he had come back via San Marco early and stood dripping with others listening to the 'battle of the bands'. Why had the cheapest café's been the best, he'd wondered: it played Rossini while the band at Florian's had catered to the world, abandoning classics for show tunes – *My Fair Lady*, Andrew Lloyd Webber – which had struck him as depressingly vulgar.

'Are you here still?' a voice said.

Now he turned to see Geraldine's brow screwed up in amusement – or was it from the sun? – as she studied him.

'I'm sorry. I'd gone elsewhere.'

'That's obvious. Want to tell me about it?'

The elf shook its head. Carine's honour said *no*. The slightly crazed, if inspired decadence of this companion put him off, while at the same time persuading him that somehow she might understand.

'I don't think I'd better,' he conceded.

'I see.' – She digested the implications (there were many), turning her profile again and giving out another sigh. 'Men do have their troubles. We were vain fools to imagine that all heartbreak and victimization belong to us women alone. For Krzysztof, I was the Don Juan, the privileged exploiter, he the sex-object who had to submit or risk committing some kind of lèse-majesté. At least that's how he saw it, or pretended to – or deceived himself into thinking so. Easy for a post-Communist to continue to interpret the world in terms of a power-struggle between the economically-deprived and their betters. Of course I fed this idea too, being too much of a designer Marxist not to recognize a certain schadenfreude in our situation. Possibly that was part of what was so erotic, maybe to both of us; because for all his Slavic gloom, Krzysztof was no shrinking violet in bed... Now, ironically, the tables are turned. I'm a relatively poor professor in Warsaw; he's "farting through silk" as he boasted the last time I saw him in one of those dreadful American phrases they pick up further east. Dresses in post-Soviet ersatz-Gucci while I wear these inspired rags. He has the usual run of Second World girlfriends whereas I'm hard-pressed to get a man to look closely enough through my wrinkles to see anything but a "pal". He exploits me, if you view fatherhood as necessitating a contribution. Not an old złoty has crossed my palm, though he appears to give some to his mother. They say the Poles, having been humiliated for two hundred years, are fatal for Westerners to take up with: their famous humour, which brought down the Reds, can only be aimed at us now. One of my friends – a gay from Milton Keynes who comes to Łódź once a year to lecture for a week – complains bitterly that there's no pleasing these people. "You'll drive yourself mad trying," he maintains; but of course, his experience is of a world where sexual exploitation's always been the norm, whether with Isherwood and Auden in Berlin or Tennessee Williams cruising Spanish Harlem with Gore Vidal.'

Tony's attention had come back through this speech. The elf had perked up – wasn't she, after all, in an invidious class-configuration with him too? Wasn't that – his wealth via Carine vs her penury due to a bohemian journey – part of the heart of the problem?

'We're all so impure,' Geraldine opined. 'Even I, in the moment he rejected me, found myself wanting to play the Sadean woman: the Donna Juana he imagined I was. Left there in the Tatras with a three-month child in womb, I had every scarlet vision – inducing miscarriage, lacerating myself via some ex-Commie abortionist, racing on further like him to the east: Ukraine, Georgia, the Caucasus, on some mad journey of experience, sleeping with Mazeppas, running guns to the Chechens, smoking a hookah on top of a mountain on the Kurdish-Armenian border. Oh, I had fantasies – women do, especially in that abandoned, no-turning-back state. But of course I lie. I could've turned back then – could still now, no doubt. There's a man in England who's loved me for twenty years, he claims. Even came to Poland searching for me once; ended up knocking up a Kraków secretary instead. Oh yes,' she concluded, 'we are all very impure…'

Tony felt himself half-recoil in distaste. Yet the elf peered out of her spongy cushion with big eyes, waiting, as it seemed, for a bedtime story of pirates. From guns in the Caucasus through images out of Lermontov or Byron, consciousness snapped back to the square where he sat; eyes travelled down the campanile which stood against the bizarre, slightly asymmetrical front of San Marco. Stars were there, gold in the mosaic blue – so many colours fluttering under an electric sky. A spirit as of corsairs had created this majesty; and if he were to travel back on his own sense of place, towards what la Serenissima had meant in tradition and still was by suggestion, wouldn't he have seen there bold men in armour? sailors on horseback cantering down the Lido? Shylocks and builders calculating in ducats? doges whipped by passions, conspirators, sexual miscreants and, amid all, men of the flesh driven to high piety and women like spirits out of Tintoretto yearning towards transcendent spaces above the Eugeanean Hills?

What was she evoking for him, this Geraldine Scott, but his own courage through her savage talent for risk?

'However, we women must settle,' she was concluding. 'Something else happens, at least while we're having kids.'

Then came a sound like the closing of huge padded doors. A clatter and a flap and the pigeons were off, flung up like a piece of spotted fabric to flutter over the scene.

Not far to the left, they came to resettle, making way for the woman as she rose suddenly and hurried away.

'There's five thousand lire – this place is so pricey – will it do? Lovely to see you. Where are you staying? – There she is. Oh!'

Shawls and skirts trailed behind her like blown feathers. Children with birdseed and parents indulgent made way like water ahead of a ship as she cut her swath across the grey pavement. Squinting into the sun, Tony searched for her goal: in the southeastern corner where the best band (Hungarian) had played, stood a small girl in a party-dress, short-sleeved, with a white lacy collar. Below pink-and-pale calves she wore a matching pair of white socks, tops folded over, above what seemed to be black patent-leather, silver-buckled shoes. Could this be so? Didn't the vision simply replicate some image out of his own childhood? some neighbour-girl he'd adored or a sister long lost?

Weren't children nowadays done up like these in the foreground: in air-soled trainers, jeans and sweatshirts decorated with stripes from their daddy's football team? – He could only marvel as a diminished Geraldine crouched, her precipitate flight coming to ground at the side of this small figure: this tiny girl next to babsia. The Polish matron rose brown out of the concentration of forms that mother and daughter comprised, cropped hair nesting in blonde curls. The child's dress was rose-coloured, he noted before Levied legs eclipsed them, then troops of khaki and – Geraldine rising – they disappeared up an alley behind the arcade, out of view.

Did they gaze back? He startled himself by realizing that, at the base of his abdomen, he felt a loss. For just as they vanished, didn't he see her bending to point him out, as if to prompt the child to take a last look at papa before waving goodbye?

Erratically, a dream recurred – had it loomed up in the night? He had been in some dusty landscape – how odd here in Venice. There had been a wild western aspect: dry-grassed plains and at the edge a stand of wind-breaking trees, eucalyptuses maybe. In the middle of this had been a gate, the border of a ranch before it gave way to fertile uplands beyond. He had just gone through it and was starting towards a copse where some cowhands on horseback were waiting to ride off. Whereto? He couldn't know yet, but through the trees and over the hill to the west the sky was blue and only vaguely mottled with cloud. Behind him he sensed some one or ones following. Turning, he saw figures, indistinct except for this same small girl, or so like her against the grey of sky and land that you could hardly distinguish a difference. 'Daddy?' did she call. Maybe, or not. But in her look, something precious momentarily held him; and it hurt him irremediably, though he knew he had to go, up to those trees, with the horses. And he had wanted to go. He was happy in the idea! Still, no decision could be taken which did not leave some other possibility behind...

He was in process of trying to interpret this night-message when he realized how hot it was getting. His brain could not focus entirely. Between potent coffee and the weight of the sun, headache and vacancy threatened. Looking around for a waiter, he had an impression of one or two dark spots on his vision. Where was his elf now? She seemed to have risen with Geraldine, vacating her soft bed of spongy matter. Meanwhile, at a table back in the shadowed arcade sat a woman of perhaps fifty, blonde and slim-legged, who might have been an incarnation of *her*, though, if so, a her transformed. This one was painting on lipstick. On the table before her sat a Gucci bag, possibly fake. Her blonde was not natural, though it may have been once. Her skin was pale, freckled at base but seemingly covered in places by make-up simulating a tan. Her black skirt was short, tight, fashionable yet too sexy for one of her age. The whole aura suggested a creature living just beyond itself: starting to inhabit those extra decades that modern existence with its vast medical 'improvements' allows, providing an end which isn't so much real living as a virtual reality.

Tony stood, slightly dazed, and, taking his cup and his bill, motioned to the waiter that he was moving into the shade. The dark spots returned as he made his way past a bandstand, empty now, it being morning still, just. Settling at the south end of Florian's portion of arcade, he realized that the dark spots were acquiring form. Two slick-suited men in sun-glasses sat immobile, staring at the square like film types of mafiosi. Effectively they eclipsed him from view of the unsettling blonde.

Why 'unsettling'? (He ordered Pellegrino.) In years past, there would have been no reason for him not to have returned her gaze had it strayed his direction. Twenty years before, perhaps even twenty-five, he had been pleased to pleasure most women. It had been an elixir to be thought attractive by those 'of a certain age', and there had been several in the period prior to Carine. Was it only because he was older now that the instinct had lapsed and all become concentrated in a single rule: not to be unfaithful to her ever, except to father a child? Of course he was not the same man he had been. He had looked young beyond youth: looked it for years in a way that a few women – fine women, if a touch timid – had considered 'romantic'. Sensing this, though not so much as to exploit it and scare them away, he had used it half-knowing – as if half-unwillingly – until the knowledge had become inevitable and the will over-conscious. Then, as he'd become visibly old enough that a young man's naïveté could no longer excuse him, the women had begun to take their revenge. They had become the Don Juans then: was there some law whereby the young man once not-young provokes timid women to be brash? Whether or no, at the moment when he'd become most vulnerable the posh blondes had struck. Like Casanova in London at age forty-three or whatever, he had met his 'Battle of Nations', to scramble the referents. Once, twice – then exile to Elba, then the Hundred Days, Waterloo and the long deterioration of St Helena… something like that. So did it happen to all men? Perhaps not quite in the same way. Still, this posh blonde, aged elf who sat at the northwestern edge of the café might have distinguished a potential john in him now, not a young rake, if she could have eyed him through the mafiosi. And she might have been a tart indeed, not posh at all but some 'white trash' relic who'd made her way here through hard graft, not being as privileged as he was, never having been saved by a Carine or male equivalent, if such incarnation existed.

Tony sighed inwardly as the waiter served his water.

'Better here in the shade,' a voice meanwhile murmured. 'I haven't seen you in years, yaani. Are you still managing to find the big picture? Shall I join you?'

The voice had an accent gentle and smooth. Tony looked to see a face round, bushy browed, a head balding with curls grisled at the sides like Persian lamb's wool. The jowls were more fleshy than he remembered. Good living shone out, though not dissipation, despite a red tinge as of weeping or hay-fever around the whites of the eyes.

The upper lip, once moustached, was shaven as clean as the cheek. A scent of eau-de-cologne mixed with aging skin evoked some benevolent father-figure from his past, though Tony couldn't specify whom. Bahadin Sohl was dressed as if in high

Harrod's: silver suit, double-breasted; exuberant display handkerchief matching blue-and-black tie descending from white collar of a puce, pinstriped shirt. A gold chain of some weight depended from a button-hole, while stubby fingers pulling out a chair sported two thick gold rings with unusual stones inlaid, shining more prominently than would be thought comme il faut on the hands of some impeccable Englishman or français.

'Be my guest,' Tony gestured.

'No, you'll be mine.' – A look passed: an 'OK' to the minders at the eclipsing table, now evidently connected with this man – a fact Tony did not find surprising.

'You look terribly prosperous,' he said.

'So do you, yaani, so do you.' – The Lebanese sat.

'Still publishing magazines?'

He half-laughed. 'Ah yes that. No, those days were a phase – for you too, I believe.'

'Not entirely. Literature's still my game – if "game" you can call it, and if that was literature.'

He had worked for a time on a fashionable glossy in London – that is, the London edition of a Parisian rag. It had not been a long 'phase', nor for him a great one; nor had it continued much after Bahadin had appeared, ostensibly to put cash into a project rapidly being killed by its editors, who failed to pay their print bills. This was back in the depths of the early 1980s recession, a 'phase' out of which the West had slowly extracted itself via two wars, the Falklands and Iran-Iraq. Being Lebanese, Bahadin had meanwhile been preoccupied then with what Menachem Begin & Co had been doing to Beirut. As a Muslim, if friendly with Maronite Christian and Druze, he had been appalled by the rape of his country and what he interpreted as the West's cynicism in supporting it. Tony of course had been sympathetic. This was shortly before his first meeting Carine. Oddly he realized now that, over the years, despite their ostensible enmity in race and religion, he had subconsciously identified this man with her – there was a similar sweet toughness.

'Do you like it here, yaani? I find it too busy. I wouldn't come to Venice if it wasn't for... They have a long tradition with us Muslims, you know – the battle of Lepanto, was it? you're a historian: you can remind me. It's nice enough, picturesque; and I like sometimes to sit at the Cipriani – you can see the sky better there. A perfect landscape always needs sky, don't you agree? This is what's wrong with Europe – too tight, too closed-in; no view. Only under a great sky can one know God. I think back to my young days in the Bekaa Valley – so celestial, peaceful. But all the Muslim world has that. There is something fine about Islam – gentle, decorative, still. Like the cool of the water in an oasis. The West doesn't know. It doesn't want to. You have no equivalent at sunset of hearing the muezzin call to prayer.'

The waiter came. Bodyguards eyed him like birds of prey as a glass of tea was set down before their master, who ignored it.

'One regrets so much when one reaches our age.' (Bahadin was older than him by a decade, Tony had always assumed, but now he realized that the difference might not be so great: a portly girth and thinning hair can disguise much.) 'In the years since we had our adventures in the magazine world, I have done many things; some perhaps not so nice.' (He recalled too how this man had once asked him to go to a middle Eastern state's cultural office to interview that country's new leader, who had later become the West's chief whipping-boy.) 'I have helped people get things they need... You look at me like that, but am I such a bad man? When your brother is killed or your land taken from you, why should you be the only one who is denied the means to fight back? It is unfair! so unfair the way the West imagines that only it or the ones it designates are to be given the power to defend themselves – or, if necessary, take revenge.'

He lifted his glass, sipped, set it down with a clack.

'You don't know, yaani. You were always too nice – the privileged type. You grew up in a secure home, had good health and looks; you were educated. What do you think it is to be a child in Gaza or Hebron, or even Amman or Cairo? And when someone like Muhammar Gaddafi comes to express the rage of the people, what do your friends in the West do? I must not reveal much; but did you know that it was the CIA who shot that police-woman in St James's Square in order to whip up reaction against Libya? That was years ago – perhaps you won't recall. It was at the start of the West's concerted effort to create another "pariah nation". They do frightful things, your people, and their Zionist friends. And we do things in reaction, and we are blamed. But who do you imagine supplies the arms to allow even our pip-squeak dictators to do what they do? Do you think Yassir Arafat could have survived all these years if the West hadn't wished it? And Saddam Hussein, that butcher – do you think we alone would have, or even could have, kept him in place?'

Tony recalled speeches like this from the Bahadin of years before. He remembered in particular a spring evening when the skies had been high and bright and they had walked together from Mayfair to Notting Hill via Hyde Park and Kensington Gardens. Though little more than a post-Punk neo-Romantic at that stage, Tony had been invited along to a penthouse in one of the great terraces overlooking the Bayswater Road. There Bahadin had introduced him to one of the smooth men who later no doubt had paved his way to the elegance and riches on show now in his clothes, rings and manner. That man had been polite, and very Westernized, apart from some constant play with worry-beads; and Tony had thought of himself as some-thing of a sophisticate to have, if even so briefly, moved in the circle of these shadowy Levantine money-men.

'Well the world turns, and it is God's will,' Bahadin was going on now, shrugging off an uprush of anger. 'Beirut is rebuilding; soon it will have so many cars and such pollution that it will look like Teheran. And of course, because people want things, I will contribute to that too. But how foolish my countrymen are! Why should they wish for what you have in L.A., or London? I should be a Bedouin tending my flock. But the Prophet goes to war if his name is insulted, if his people are put down or Allah is taken in vain. And so when the West gave us Salman Rushdie, whom it paid and protected, we had to respond with the fatwa. And when the West denied arms to our brothers in Bosnia while supplying Orthodox Serbs and Catholic Croats to the teeth – even from the rusting tankers you can see in this port – what did they expect us to do? And not only expect; what did they *want* us to do? Because no arms industry can grow rich without dealers. And no dealer can deal unless some sense of outrage is stirred. And no sense of outrage is stirred unless someone goes around saying that the world, or at least some part of it, is very unfair… Yaani, we are terrible people, you and I. We sit here complacent, living off it, part of it, whether we know it or not. Every corner, every shifting border, every choke-point on the globe where two or more religions or philosophies or language groups meet, there are the evil men stirring. The Balkans, Horn of Africa, the Mahgreb, Palestine, the Persian Gulf, Caucasus, Pakistan vs India, the southeastern Asian borderlands, Central America in not so distant days, Northern Ireland – even, when I knew you last, the Falklands…'

And who was doing the stirring, he almost asked. But being up on conspiracy theories (God knew, since the death of Diana, the world was as awash in them as in his formative years amid shootings of two Kennedys), Tony had a fair notion of where all this might be leading.

'And now they are at it in Kosovo, yaani – just across the Adriatic. Why do you think we are here?'

'"We"?' Tony challenged.

'But you are waiting for someone.' – Bahadin changed tack. 'I've been talking too much. You must think I am rude.'

'Not at all,' he smiled, though there would be something odd, he could see, about being found here conversing with such an overt enemy (or was he?) of some of Carine's associates.

'You were always a disappointment,' the other sighed, half-tracking his train-of-thought. 'You could see the big picture. You understood and yet – you have stayed with them, haven't you?'

'Who?'

'Your own group of thugs, instead of ours.'

At that moment something happened:

Beyond the two Florentine profiles of the minders, the

blonde woman stood. Like them, she was wearing darkglasses – so Tony noted in peripheral vision. The jet-blackness of the frames gave an illusion that she was wearing a black hat as well, though all that was on her head was hair dyed like straw with a sugar coating. Raising her bag, she left her table and strode towards them. Her fitted jacket was yellow with thick, round plastic buttons that matched in jetness her too-short skirt, below which she wore netted tights. These details Tony did not quite fully take in as she grew large in the background, behind the guards. She was only a radiant blur at this stage: the visual equivalent of the sound of a bumble-bee approaching. Perhaps no one noticed her more than subliminally: Bahadin's back was turned and the profiles of the thugs set as silhouettes of condottieri on Renaissance coins. Only when she passed their table did a feature stir: one of the pair's cheeks began to twitch, as if some sensory receptor had been activated. She continued to cross. Her hips, not unshapely despite age, swayed enough to draw an eye and reanimated Tony's sense of the elf as one jostled the edge of his table. It made Bahadin's glass of tea tilt. Three things then occurred: she reached out a hand to right the teetering vessel; he, Bahadin, looked up in alarm; the two protecting knights rose out of their seats and, like secret servicemen shielding the President, inserted themselves between her and their master. Tony gaped; the woman eyed Bahadin unreadably, a shade of a smile revealing bad teeth, while Bahadin's own eyes in their red rims swam through unknown oceans of fear, anger and begging for mercy, or maybe redemption. The two mafiosi, as if ashamed at their performance, froze like statues. Casting a look of contempt at them, shade of her smile vanishing, the women looked briefly at Tony as if to say, 'You keep lousy company.' She then continued on her way out of Florian's and down the arcade, until she had buzzed out of sight into a crowd of tourists in front of the doge's palace.

What did it mean?

Tony's eyes lingered on the spot where she'd vanished. Meanwhile, around him the down-flutter of righting cups and resettling nerves carried on. His uninvited companion was distracted for long enough that he could track in his mind's eye others walking away: women he had loved, all merging into Carine, but a Carine as she had been in earlier incarnations, hips boyish, the elf having flit back as it were to inhabit her. He recalled a moment shortly after they'd met when he'd been playing music at whatever flat or house-sit he'd been living in. It had led to discussion of what kind of music she liked and, though dedicated to rock-n-roll then, as ever, she had answered, to impress him, 'O Schönberg, Schopenhauer – that sort of thing.' He had teased her by asking what piece of Schopenhauer's was her favourite, to which, suddenly aware of her error, she had blushed a deep rose and, summoning the dog who was her inseparable companion in those days, said, 'Come on, Razz; we'd better go.' Years later, when they'd had a row in the Coliseum bar, possibly over how much she'd been drinking, there being considerable stress in her business at the time, it had ended with her marching out of the theatre and up St Martin's Lane looking for a cab – non-existent in central London at that hour. He'd followed her at a distance, protective, as she'd made her long circuit through Covent Garden and down to the Strand where, lacking a cab still, she'd stood shivering waiting for the Number 11 bus. To this day he could still hear the clack of her heels on that pavement. So slim and vulnerable had her hips seemed, and the thin arms clutched in at the elbows, that he had wondered with fond anguish if she were going to end up like some character out of an Anita Brookner novel, unmanned and single into darkest middle-age, until she had reached apotheosis as an arthritic yet terribly bright-eyed spinster. Carine, however, had shown remarkable verve. Her ability to turn most situations to good, to wait out altercations until he (or whoever) had come round; her chutzpa to make a scheme succeed against all odds, had allowed her to grow in her pretentionless way while others had faded. She had become *someone*, despite (or perhaps because of) her innate vulnerability. And now as she sat in respected state in some posh meeting-room at the Danieli, elves who had radiated wild powers in youth grew embittered, or at best frangible in their attractiveness, as they jostled glasses in San Marco Square, in order to make some obscure point or just gain attention or perhaps merely because their slightly malnourished pins were no longer as steady as they might have been following an unwitnessed ingestion of pills, washed down by spirits, along with a cheapest-on-the-menu tot of café. The great love-women, he recalled reading (was it in Lawrence again?), lose their allure at forty or fifty and turn greyish, avid, into real grimalkins, prowling for prey that becomes increasingly scarce. No matter how elegant their dress or clever their chat, it could hardly disguise how they'd gone to pieces as human beings, so that what had begun as as ravishing as an English garden in spring would end by seeming artificial, if in flower at all. And whatever sweet tones one might've once heard out of unpainted lips now masked a keen mumbo-jumbo of witches distantly stirring a pot.

Bahadin, he realized, was lamenting in this vein too:

'This is how a man may end up, yaani – with a woman of a certain age out to get him. Don't think I am suffering paranoia: it's more than that. I have seen it with others – I feel it myself and must admit that in some strange way it may be God's will. I have a wife: she is my third. I wish I could tell you it wasn't so; but… I am a man, and things happen. My first wife was a fine and beautiful Muslim girl from my home town. We grew up together; our fathers were friends. It was a good marriage – good for business reasons, politics, religion. Her people were powers in the Bekaa Valley; together our families were important throughout the Lebanon, and we had many shops. I loved her as well, which is not always so in these arrangements: we had our first child when I was nineteen; then another and after some time two more. Then, as happens with some middle-Eastern women, she grew fat. This is no sin, and I as a man know that real women do not have to look like skeletons of a kind you and I used to put into our magazine. But along with her weight she grew, not discontent or lazy exactly, but into something other than the girl I had loved. And of course I was still relatively young.'

He paused. The minders, returned to their table, had again become as if living medallions of warriors of the seicento; or, more prosaically, Tony thought, models for suits or designer specs from one of a half-dozen Italian fashion-houses.

'You knew me at that time, yaani. I blame the war – why would I have been in London if the Israelis and Syrians were not ripping apart our world in Beirut? But whatever is to blame – and I did not have to give into temptation – I fell into sensual ways. You recall. There were girls – the magazine attracted them. We were little better than pimps, the editors and I; you let us deceive you into thinking you were writing your "arts" page for art's sake when in fact the idea was to seduce investors, go to parties, put people's faces in gossip columns – other people's faces: the ones whom the snobbish English with their *Tatler & Queen's* wouldn't then stoop to, though they were glad to take our cash. I'm speaking of Arabs and Muslims worldwide; of Nigerian black men and those from Malaysia, Indonesia, Brunei. You worked for us only for an issue or two: you did not see how it went. You did not see who we were catering for finally, nor go out on the yachts, nor play with the young ladies with small minds and large curves who inevitably hung around. I am not proud of it. So why do I make this confession? and what have I to confess? A man is a man. The Prophet had many wives. The surest of all ladders to the Divine is the ladder of love; and no man's imagination, to write verses or make deals, can travel like it ought to unless stimulated by his manhood – yes, yaani, this thing we have below here.'

Tony was both flattered and unsettled. Why did people single him out to tell tales to? Was he becoming universally recognizable as one of life's eunuch-observers? There was the problem too of Carine's imminent arrival. Of course he did not feel perfect about her turning up while he sat with this unexpected confessee whose foot-soldiers were only a half-step away. But there was more. He wanted to be ready for her. He loved her, after all; and after the row in the night, he wanted to be settled enough in mind to be able to devote himself to her entirely. So here was the rub. In the ebb and flow of past minutes his elf had disappeared, if only momentarily, and he felt – was it coffee? the Danieli's breakfast? – a pain deep in the chest. Somehow it was plain that the origin of this was not just physical. Though unable to think uninterruptedly, he imagined the pain to have come up half because he had not got his mind set; had not worked up his spirits adequately to suppress the disintegrative elements. So as Bahadin now recited the history of his later affairs, Tony grew nervous that – despite the odd warnings, blonde grimalkin and so on – something *other* was lurking: some odd perversity that threatened to inundate him like the lagoon overflowing the square, or an unremissioned disease.

Bahadin did not seem to notice him retreating inwards. 'My story,' he went on, 'is not so different from that of any man of my type... I had money – more and more of it. (Money is not hard to come by, yaani, once you've begun.) I went out; I owned things; I was a man-about-town – so it is natural that the "ladies" with titles or a taste for jewels yet nothing but an overdraft should buzz around me. We have all watched the Duchess of Fergie and Lady Rain Cartland. It is a vulgar world; yet how is a poor wog from the Bekaa Valley supposed to resist? – So my second wife... My first one wailed like a widow mourning a lost son; my children looked at me as if I had become some filthy Greek libertine. We lived in a grand house in Paris near the Bois, and within six months I was fed up, and within twelve I was with an East European blonde half my age... And now, yaani? Of course she too has left me, or I her, minus another million, but – what is money finally?'

Tony's attention came back on this phrase. He was about to insert a word when Bahadin sighed and repeated,

'What is money?' – He drained his glass, then answered himself: 'Money is a sixth sense without which the other five aren't much use – isn't that what one of your fine authors once wrote? Money? it is all I have left – my talent for making it, to give to my children, whatever their mother persuades them to think of their terrible daddy.'

On this he seemed resolved, though to his listener's mind it sounded like an imposed conclusion: a compensatory stab at a faith by a man who had become more and more désillusioné. Still, it allowed him to rise from his seat.

'But I have demanded too much of your time, yaani. You are meeting with someone; I won't embarrass you by overstaying. In any case' – here he nodded to his men, one of whom motioned to the waiter while slipping out a wallet, 'we too have appointments: business, not pleasure – though I'll tell you a secret, and I hope you'll remember when you think of your friend Bahadin… However dismayed you become with life or love, never show it – except perhaps, as in this case, to someone you trust who you are unlikely to see again. And whatever business you throw yourself into, make it a pleasure – or try to make it appear so to the world – even if, on analysis, it is terrible. Because life is terrible, yaani. We all die in the end. The point is to make it seem glorious as we waste away.'

With that he was off, up the northwest stretch of arcade, in the direction opposite to the one in which the blonde had vanished and Carine was meant to appear. He seemed to grow taller in relation to the guards on either side of him, following a few steps behind. Back straight, head erect, Bahadin seemed to personify pride while they seemed somewhat hunched, as if by professional deformation. A kind of primal tableau of manhood vanished with the trio down through the arches. It echoed other eras and ways of being, which may have helped to create these arches in the first place, or at least the ducats to build the galleys to make the ducats through trade to make the ducats to build the warships to protect that trade and the churches and houses and work-of-art, synagogues and mosques and nuclear bombs, glossy magazines, call-girls and extravagant yachts… But *what* was he thinking, our man chastised himself. Was he attracted to that world after all? a world he had perhaps flirted with once yet had turned his back on, to no regret? Or had he regret secretly? Hadn't every man, really? Wasn't every Italian male supposed to long in his heart to be a mafia capo?

Unsettling himself by this scrap of idea, he redirected his attention to the south end of the square, from where Geraldine and her child had disappeared to where the cathedral arose to the corner in which Carine was still nowhere to be seen. It was five minutes, seven minutes past the appointed hour. 'I promise not to be late today,' she had said; 'we'll have lunch wherever you want, so no blood sugar crises!' But of course she'd be late. She always was, pleading work, the plea usually being valid. Nowadays the world was divided between those who had too much work and those who had too little, and gradually through the years Carine had become the first while he the second. Was this why his mind tended to wander while hers remained so simple and sure? Was it just circumstance that made us as we were, Bahadin rich yet angry, Geraldine brilliant yet in tatters potentially? or could there be something deep in the genes, some tendency in the 'racial memory' – of Carine's Jewish family-in-trade, for example – which made her work tirelessly while he, Tony, had settled in mid-life into this demi-character out of James? – No sooner had the thought risen than he experienced a sharp, fiery pang of rebellion. Because there was something in him of the pirate of Pound, wasn't there? of Bahadin and Geraldine too: some terrible, wonderful flame of the life-force still burning? – The elf turned on a tap and out shot a jet. Yellow, red, blue, shimmering at the edges in distortions, it burned uninvited, frighteningly enlivening to his pleasurable pain. And out of it as if out of a burning bush before his vision, he could see her approach – oh, how he wished it were Carine! but it wasn't. It was *her* again, and he knew he was lost: so wildly in thrall to whatever, whomever she was, that it was all he could do to hold himself down in his seat; not to run through the arcade to the nearest phone and dial her – the number of the flat she was sleeping in over a shop – and tell her he loved her, loved her, loved *her*! And why hadn't he done so? Why hadn't he tried more? Why hadn't he gone to bed with her? What in him was so perverse as to have made him resist? what vengeful, suppressive, puritan gene?

He was drunk with her. His tongue felt thick, wet, aching with desire to lick her, like some sad dog. She was his bitch in heat. An overwhelming scent seemed to draw him halfway over a continent towards her. He imagined her parts and was cunt-drunk without ever having seen them. But... this was madness! He hated himself. How could one conjure up such images? He loved Carine, and yet... there it was. He had tried to deny it. But he was in love – or 'in lust', as they say: anyhow clearly in thrall. And now as the surge passed – the ache in the abdomen, loins, bowels – he felt breathless and as if he might even pray to some deity unknown to deliver him from this fury and back to a quiet life. But then... 'I want you to be the father of my child,' came her whisper. And: 'You're a kind man.' And later: 'You're sweet.' And later still: 'I think you're very generous.' – Words, mere words! only prettily, lovingly stated. And so perilous.

Breathlessness continued. He felt like a creature fighting for its life. What could he think of to dampen this suffusion? this fear of what a woman of her kind might do, to him, to *them*? But... he'd been through this and, besides, what was 'a woman of her kind'? Not Geraldine Scott. Not one of Bahadin's girls, nor of his later wives either. She was an elf: *his* elf – his guardian-angel perhaps? tormenting demon? He didn't know. He could not make her out, passing back through the flames... Then a stratagem came. Concentrate on some less attractive feature: her feet, which were webbed slightly – though what Lorelei or Undine has ever been loved for her feet? likewise her legs, which were a touch knock-kneed, as if drawn by Beardsley. But... her lips were full and breasts warm: he had to rush over them and concentrate on her hips, which were skeletal and not really for child-bearing. She was not built to be a mother, no! not the mother of his long-imagined child, whatever her pixie self said. But... was that the last word?

The stratagem half-working, heat subsided for long enough that he could sit back half-weary into the sweat of the day. But... her skin: it was pear-white (a flash of imagining her nude: the sore cleft of lips cut raspberry-mauve across yellow-pink, oh!)

Suppressing himself into recalling her poverty – the cheap sheen of her trousers, the waif-like hang of her jacket over shoulders hunched and ill-postured back... he remembered her claim that her mother had beaten her as a child. Didn't all Cockney and working-class women in those days, he wondered, hazy in recall from when he'd first gone to London, drizzling grey: a London he'd seemed to have known for centuries, perhaps because of some teenaged reading of Dickens. And was *that* it? In the soul of his attraction was there some deep-buried, missionary zeal? some schadenfreude or sentimental yearning to link with the beaten-down heart of the race? some weird desire to raise it? to create a grand lady, goddess, duchess or queen, like Cophetua with the Beggar Maid?

He had seen her once with blonde wisps pulled back, exposing the line of her cheek. The face's sculpture had been strong, almost crude, yet the aura remained of a crystalline sylph. Her nose had appeared bulb-like yet went half-visible between diamonds of eyes and pomegranate timbre of lips. And the contour... she was aging but, strange to say, what had been etched by time seemed only to contribute to a sense that she'd been born long, long ago in some myth; that she had lived many lifetimes through legend only now to arrive for a last incarnation, like a starchild to produce a starchild for him.

But Carine! (*She* would not let go: the ruby lips fading stole a kiss, and he'd said, 'You're braver than me,' as she'd gathered her things in the café where they'd met and seen lying there, damp on the floor, two umbrellas, collapsed yet unrolled; of which, following his eyes, she'd murmured, 'Our umbrellas have had a better time than we have'; so that now he recalled, at last, the feature that had most entranced him – how serendipitously clever she was.) But Carine... How could he do this to *her*?

It was not her fault that she could no longer have a child. Of course she had lived a raucous youth – drink, drugs and no rest – but who hadn't? Of course they should never have had the abortion; but what would her father have said, let alone his, if a child had been born out of wedlock? And who hadn't had an abortion in those days? They had been young then: it had been 'too early'. Who was to have known it would have come to seem as it did? that she would fall ill in time? All the bizarre diseases swirling around the globe nowadays, bacteria weaving through hermetic tubes of airplanes, tuberculosis, pneumonia – who was to have known that infection would attack her and force them, force her over an ocean of tears, to allow them to take out her womb? So that now she could never have the child she had longed for. And he couldn't have it with her – couldn't have offspring at all unless... But, he couldn't leave her – no! He'd been through this. How could you leave someone you'd loved all those years, especially after everything she had been through?

He sat glum in the heat.

It wasn't just that he was wed to her money and success, as the world, or some part of it, thought. Whatever the world thought, he was not just the exploitative male wife of a female arch-magnate – was he?

Weariness overtook him as, staring dead into the corner she was meant to appear out of, he felt himself slide into a post-caffeine trance.

'I might've guessed I'd find you here,' a voice said; and now it was figure out of his deeper past that arose.

An aura of dark eyes, brown hair and compact form alighting on the chair alongside him. It might have been a Parisian stage radical of the 1960s from the sense of nervous, perpendicular spirit it gave off. A face flushed from the heat, eyes protuberant as if with some uncanny power (or was it just unbalanced diet?), a voice nasal, high yet seeming half-whispered, spouting agitated yet confidential greeting in words almost too lucid and neat – who was this diminutive demon? some mass-murderer in potential? an out-of-work agent provocateur?

He gave off an impression of inordinate self-belief, as if he thought himself the genuine conscience of mankind, or at least Tony Thomas. What made him so sure of himself, so as if he'd known the Great Scheme of Things since the Origin of Time, however foreign the setting? What was he posing as now? architect? itinerant rogue? descendent of some weird strain of 18th century freemasonry? – Distantly, Tony recalled a wild boy he had gone to school with and known later in drop-out days. What had he been then? a pot-pusher? petty smuggler? Too intelligent for his own or anyone else's good, he had always managed to radiate the insight of the defiant, the ferocious – a terrible type! Despite the heat here, he was still wearing the leather jacket of the would-be tough guy. Yet where was his wife now, Tony eccentrically wondered; or had he gone gay in the meantime? It had never been easy to locate a centre in this sinister, yet curiously erect persona: this macho emanation who, unlike Bahadin, had so little of the gentleman about him yet somehow, at base, seemed more civilized, more clean and oddly in tune with itself.

'Are you – ?'

'Yes of course. Are you surprised? Why shouldn't I turn up in Venice like you? The world doesn't belong only to the posh, you know, mate.'

He had a shade of Carine in him as well, though ghastly transformed. He was the elf with gender adulterated and magic switched off. He was Bahadin in potential for resentment, Geraldine in rashness of courage, an excrescence of London 'hip' mixed the American road of the 1950s or barricades that once had transformed Venice, Italy, Europe, the world into the beginnings of what it was now, or part of still or would become – a real 'democracy', a scrambling of each among all, a carnival or famine-time of every man for himself. Through this odd creature, who was both a younger self and scourge of his present, Tony glimpsed characters out of books he had once admired, from Julien Sorel to Jack London's sad Cockney underman, Mugridge. Merging with pale ghosts of rock-stars from past decades, they shadowed what was shooting up in consciousness here in the crucial midday.

'You're at decision-time, bud,' the other mused as a sheet of fantasy fell like a theatrical scrim to reveal his old companion and alter ego as he had been in WASP class-lists of their youth, Curt Clayton Burnham III. 'Maybe I should describe it as "decision time again"?'

Most Americans of their age had become easy, relaxed – at least in outer demeanour. It was one of the hallmarks of the great republic, in contrast to other nations. Off in 'big sky country' where 'a man is a man' (and women too, often) the limbs thickened and pace slowed and eyes took on a glaze as of viewing pale heavens: as if the whole trajectory of a 'good life' were towards some progressive fulfilment which, if a man hadn't attained it by middle-age, he'd better pretend he had and pretend long enough that he'd come to believe his own bullshit. Well... that let out this devil. Did it let Tony out too? Weren't they twin dissident faces of the tribe? the Pound and Eliot – or, if not that by some distance, at least the outlaw and exile?

'You look as degenerate as ever, Curtis,' he mused.

The other shrugged. 'And you as self-satisfied, bro'.'

There was a hint of a smile as if among friends, though none of the wide sunniness or back-slappery which would have ranked as the norm among ordinary specimens of a type that blessed numberless high school reunions.

'I imagine,' the guest said, ordering café concetto, 'that the current *crise* Tony Thomas has something to do with whether it can be right to stay a kept man. Or is it whether "a man" should continue to lead a life in "ornamental exile", or both?'

Tony retorted: 'Does the fact that you haven't shaved this "a.m." give you some god-ordained right to be impertinent?'

'Come off it,' the other grinned. 'You're glad I've shown up out of nowhere – we both know it. You need me.'

This was true, at least in part.

'So is the brief at this stage,' Tony played on, 'for you to tell me entirely unknowing what's wrong with my existence and how to put it right?'

Burnham chuckled. 'The trouble with you is the trouble with me, man.'

'What? too clever by half?'

'The divided self.'

'That's the definition of an intellectual, isn't it? A person who can sustain two or more conflicting trains-of-thought at the same time.'

'Some might say it's the definition of a schizophrenic.'

'Some might. But in that case, which one of us is the ego and which the id?'

'Maybe you should go back to Nietzsche, pal. Apollo and Dionysus would be more flattering. Or are you ready at last to come into the real world and recognize us both as a couple of dead Beats?'

'You mean deadbeats or, say, Cassady and Kerouac?'

He chuckled. 'I've read that study of yours.'

'Which?'

'The one that says that the beatniks were step-grandkids of Henry James, begotten by Henry Miller.'

Tony had forgotten that he'd come up with such aperçus. Having dislocated his previous life recently, he was not wholly unpleased to be reminded of it, though it hardly solved his problems. Indeed, it might have worsened them. Did Curt know as much via one of his odd flares of insight? Was that what made him so weirdly threatening? A penchant for threat, Tony recalled, was a quality he'd once revelled in. And wasn't it just that – the old link to danger – that had been missing in his life in recent years? Wasn't that what had made him prey to the lure of the elf? and if so, didn't his responses to the lure represent in some way a 'final chance'? Yet what was the lure to? life? destruction? both at once? Schizophrenia, indeed. Existence was riven into the compulsion to risk and the recoil towards comfort: into the faith to dare all and the will to risk nothing.

'Don't disappear on me quite yet,' his companion quipped; and shortly he proceeded to unravel a tale.

This had to do with the landscape of Western America – California, Arizona, even some forays across the border into Mexico. It included mention of that wife, and perhaps one or two further; also a child, or children – the text was hard-bitten, yet vague. Mostly, it had to do with a reality of experience that was dry, isolate but somehow matey all at once. The man had

seen the inside of pool-halls and jails; he sought to seem endless-
ly vital, at least in rhetoric. However, at the end of each clipped
episode came the snap of a zippo or puff of a cough, indicating
that the antinomian life had been taking its toll.

It intrigued Tony Thomas. Was his double across the table
living or dying? – On account of his size, Burnham had always
seemed youthful: a mascot in high school, puer eternus as adult.
Now at forty-seven or eight surely, he was showing signs of the
skull under the skin. The gums were bad, the hair unable to hide
its recession even in a beneficent Venetian humidity. The slim
fingers looked rheumatic and, if he hadn't been wearing leather
on an eighty degree day, the forearms might have shown themselves as no longer quite up to defending their possessor in the
tried-and-true, Hollywoodish ritual of fists.

'I think I may have less chance of disappearing first in the
long run,' Tony observed without aggression.

'Maybe physically, sport. Good food, cushy life – true, I
haven't had them. But at least I won't die of the Hamlets.'

'The what?'

'Indecision. Not knowing when to fuck Ophelia or stab the
king.'

He recalled how, on his first trip to Europe, this alter ego,
though gleefully scoffing at the 'fop-fag' continent, had been
Virgil to his Dante. In those days, descent had been via hash-
ish, sexual mélange and a cult of the wandering backpack; but
one half-legitimate lay-by had lured him – out of rock-n-roll
intrigue he had been seduced into theatre and for a season had
cavorted with actors hoping for bit parts in fringe productions
of Shakespeare. In the end, all that came had been adoption in
word, if not image, of a callow Machiavellianism such as the
Bard himself had purloined from Christopher Marlowe.

'I see. So you're still my preceptor in how to act?'

'Maybe. If you still long for a midsummer night's dream
'fore it's too late.'

The irony, of course, was that he *did* have insight. It was
one thing to listen to a Geraldine or Bahadin: their tales leant

his problems a certain context, but they had no power to see into his soul as it were – only someone quite similar whom he'd known all his life had a chance to do that, and not just any someone but a kind of twin. The pitfall was that a twin might see too much – so many details of the big picture – that the few items he left out became correspondingly crucial: i.e., the closer he got to the truth, the more likely his 'answer' might just miss the mark. And often just missing can bring greater disaster than missing by a long shot or not shooting at all.

'You were always adept, Curtis, at getting it wrong.'

'You don't like me, do you?'

'It's not that,' he returned.

'Yes it is. You're afraid of me – afraid I'll get too near the heart of the matter. That's why you went away, isn't it? You're not an expat out of the spirit of adventure; otherwise you'd've gone to South America or East Asia like me. Safety's your thing; protecting yourself. That's why you're living in Europe as a plump capon with a hen to cluck over you, and all the people you've ever loved or could love really pass through your consciousness like ghosts.'

'What are you driving at?'

'Why don't you go home?'

'Why should I? Europe's the future. It's also the past – a real one, a rich one. I don't see why it shouldn't be my present. I've beaten out my exile.'

'Maybe. And lost your way.'

What was this? mere chauvinism? his American face mocking him? 'Why don't *you* go home?' he wanted to shout back but instead put the obvious: 'What are you doing here?'

Burnham shrugged. 'Talking to you.'

'Talking at me, true. Hardly to me.'

He smirked. 'Have it your way. But if everything's so fucking right with your life, why are you barking at me?'

Tony motioned the waiter and gazed at his watch. Carine was late now by twenty minutes. It was time to go look for her.

'I'm sorry if I've been "barking",' he growled to the uninvited guest, whose presence he could not wholly disdain. 'Maybe it's the heat.'

'If it's too hot, man, get out of the kitchen.'

It always amazed him how his countrymen, even the most appealing of them, ended by dealing in portentous clichés. 'I won't ask what that means. Are you going to tell me?'

Burnham shrugged again. He seemed tired suddenly, like a preview of some wizened sage – say, the miscreant Pound – and for a moment Tony felt a flare of something akin to compassion. For a moment, life came back his direction filled with old intimates like this. For a time, he agreed with the other's apparent conclusion: that his way had become that of a Jamesian capon – grand, but infertile. Wasn't it true, after all, that he was now a kept man, half-mothered, with no real profession but giving the occasional lecture or writing the odd book that few shops would carry and fewer readers buy? Wasn't this all his type could hope for by uprooting to Europe, yet not sinking roots? The old 'man without a country' syndrome stared out at him, from Pound's grizzled visage, from James's Caesarian crown. Then the elf arose, like some spirit-form – some ectoplasmic emission out of what he was not, or not yet quite, but feared to become.

She took shape again, this time like a Tinkerbell out of J. M. Barrie. She darted around his skull trailing star-dust until, in a swirl and a swish, she vanished from sight – flash! as in a moment of heatstroke – and through a gleam in Burnham's dark eye, bore into another host psyche. And this was an explanation, wasn't it? To have *her* meant to become *him* in some way. And to become him meant to accept what he'd so artfully dodged: his real life, native destiny, rough, unrefined, canny and perhaps immature finally. The animal was here, basic man, creature of the woods and the wits and of mortal withering. He had been well-fed, well-nurtured. He had given himself progressively to a civilization of comfort and high culture, not 'counter' at all. This he had esteemed. Mostly he had never doubted, or doubted for long, that his steps towards fine exile had marked out a triumph: a victory of escape from the 'air-conditioned nightmare'.

And here in Venice, this living museum – free not of tourists but at least of the ubiquitous auto pollutants – is where it could end: where it *would* do so if he took care and didn't watch out. That was the message. It would end here at best, or something implied by it. And could he stand that? to be a museum-piece, an odd footnote not even inscribed on a grave stone in San Michele? Or? Or – ? What was the *or*?

'I never wanted to become like you,' he murmured.

'Nor I like you,' the other replied.

'But I do miss it sometimes.'

'Miss what?'

'The life I've imagine you've had.'

'And I yours, man. And I yours… Wanna swap?'

It was said with a grin – a grin exposing American dentistry: hyper-cleaned, straightened teeth which, despite eroding gums, seemed to defy and at the same time emphasize that skull. His own teeth needed cleaning, but they were sound. And was that an answer to this latest sally? why he did not 'wanna swap' (or did he?) A lure of whitened teeth could never make up for a certainty that, teeth white or yellowed, one could live in the mix: in the fertile compost of Time that was Europe – that *would be* Europe – despite the American car, at least so far as until this serene majesty by the sea vanished beneath her lagoon.

'Ever show you these?' Burnham asked, lighting a last fag, as the waiter collected from Tony for drinks.

'Show me what?'

Four worn-edged photographs passed over the table. Out of a wallet came the cliché of high school reunions – who was it? some girl? Tony needed his glasses to see… a lost sister? ex-wife? She had unaged. Looking back through the sequence, there was a bride before bag-pipes, a hippy wandervögel, a child on her bottom having fallen off her bike, a babe in arms. There was his beloved, or someone's: Carine and the elf; one and the other inseparable, fused. The child Tony had longed for this devil had apparently had – Geraldine's Agnieszka across the square – but at what cost?

Now he stood. Burnham had shrunk to seem more roden-
tine than ever in his evil seat: a wild, stubbled, yet partly triumphant Mephisto. Tony muttered a few words, to which he
replied:

''s OK, man. No excuses. I've known what it is to be pussy-
whipped.'

On which offensive and not-quite-accurate stab at a more
intimate 'truth', half designed to be matey, our incipiently portly protagonist took flight.

He thought he heard a voice calling behind but didn't look
back. Sure footfalls led him quickly down the arcade, away from
a resounding 'Hey man, wait for me!' and then more worrying
'Don't leave me like this!' For a flash he saw in his mind's eye
the man not being able to right himself, struggling to get out of
his chair. But Tony could not turn round – or could he? In his
inner eye, he was too sure of a grey-haired, wild-eyed alter ego
trying to pursue him; he hardly needed to glance back to see if
it were dragging a leg or stretching an arm out, as if in supplica-
tion. Clap-clap went the heels of the Bally sandals Carine had
bought him at Heathrow. Flap-flap went the Bennetton trousers
over their polished cross-hatches. Flip-flop went a straw-col-
oured blazer in the breeze made by his dash over the lip of the
Molo. Out of the sun, into another gallery he dove, swimming
between tourists, the tackiest kind, disgorged off vaporetti rock-
ing beside the Riva in front of the Danieli. Black men sold plastic
bags pretending to be leather; a smoother type of Albanian ped-
dled sun-glasses, jesters' caps, post cards, souvenirs. A festival
atmosphere smiled on the horde, a smile somewhat too wide,
displaying decayed teeth. Up six stone steps and over a bridge he
traversed, the canal snaking below in behind the famous Leads.
Here was the statue of Casanova, a last great Venetian, the ami-
able rogue who had escaped the prison, victim of a hypocriti-
cal, soon-to-be-crushed Inquisition, to career across a continent
with other rogues, imposters, ersatz-aristos, venal servants, har-
lots and egregious grand dames in thrall to bizarre metaphysics.
The classical libertine held two canines by a lead; their upper

bodies bore human breasts and heads topped with powdered wigs. So was this what one arrived at by escaping one's past? someone else's more 'festive' grotesquery?

Tony turned heel. Curt Burnham: where was he? Neither stroke-stricken nor whole could he be glimpsed in the crowd. Should one go back and search for him? What had possessed him to race off so? what horror had lurked?

The elf wasn't here, he realized as he slipped into the revolving door of the Danieli and received the 'Buongiornos' of the green-liveried operatives who served the high-blown banditti. His room-key was in place; there was an envelope in the box – for Carine doubtless: who'd send him a message here? Ignoring it, he carried on through the lobby, experiencing gradually the relief of its coolness and freedom from crowds under too much midday sun. The atmosphere hushed. Though he loathed this hotel and would have preferred some albergo or even a rented room, he had to admit that its noble loggia and grand staircase were calming, muffling his agitation, bringing peace from an epoch when elegant princes had enjoyed the best of civilization in the olden republic. For most of the occupants of these sofas and chairs, the dark high room denoted safety, not the tortures of the Counterreformation or conspiracies on back stairs. The wails of the condemned in the Leads or swarm of water-rats in deeper dungeons disturbed not a thought for a couple from Tucson padding by in gaudy golf duds (where on earth in Venice did one play golf?) or a family from Osaka sorting bits of shopping from one designer bag to another. Not a shadow of Aschenbach disturbed the vision of two Rotterdam dames inquiring at reception the best way to the Lido; nor did the tall Jewish man from Manhattan entertain a dream or a fear about Shylock or Sir Ferdinand Klein as he made his way up, briefcase in hand, to a business lunch on the roof. – Was consciousness a curse then or font of greater riches? The question returned, the same question in a way, about division: the division he had earned through a lifetime of education, culture and sensibility. Could a man live fully – that is, fulfilledly – by this or by that:

an innocuous, half-conscious existence well-lived in the sense of families, babies, etc., or a wedding for better or worse to the 'monuments of unaging intellect', the centuries of grandest taste? Here in the Danieli both were set cheek-by-jowl: the ancient rooms out of Titian or Veronese; the vulgar rich of the moment being catered for by near thugs, sons of the sons of the cut-throats who had got and preserved the lucre of Danieli and kind in the first place... So his thoughts ran as, by indirection, he spied in a corner tucked under the loggia his darling Carine, sipping champagne.

The picture was easy, predictable, innocent. On the sofa beside her sat the colleague whom we have agreed to call Edmund. Lank, sandy-haired, soft-faced behind wire-rimmed specs, he was smiling at a long-nosed Renaissance type in a suit who was explaining some matter to a small group – sub-group of the larger bund convoked here. There were five or six present, wrapping up loose ends from the morning plenary session or deciding a strategy for tomorrow. Was Tony annoyed? – He stood in the susurrus gazing. Would Carine turn? Would she get up and rush over, trailing behind explanations, bearing apologies for being late by more than a half-hour? Did it matter? – He waited. They all nodded in silence, engrossed. Whatever business was at hand, he saw without effort – without the humiliation of having to go over and ask, interrupting, impressing on their consciousnesses, these other men's, what he was or wasn't, what by contrast they were or weren't, for the umpteenth time – that it was important: it was money, her money, their ease; too important for him to do other than turn back and fade from the scene, off through the lobby and out the revolving-door.

'Prego, Signor Bleistein?' one of the concierges called.

They had checked in by Carine's family name, still in use (and of use) for 'professional purposes'. There had been no fuss to point out that his surname was Thomas, and indeed hers via marriage. So 'Signor Bleistein' it had become.

'Allora, a package has arrived here for you, but it is by the wrong name – or the right one? Your wife was passing the desk when the lady arrived and asked for "Mr Thomas". She took it and asked me to leave it here for you.'

'Who?'

'Your wife, signor,' answered the concierge, middle-aged, efficient, gazing at his customer a touch sceptically.

'I mean, what woman,' Tony returned. 'Who delivered whatever it is?'

Swivelling, the man removed the packet from its cubby-hole and passed it over the desk. Releasing it, he poised the heels of his palms on the polished hardwood between them.

'A woman,' he shrugged. 'English? German? She spoke Italian a little. Hair so; a shawl.'

Geraldine? And had met Carine? But what was *that* about, he wondered, nodding thanks, going out and looking down at what was in his hand – book evidently, paperback by weight.

He didn't stop to unwrap it. In the heat and the crowd he sauntered back towards the square, trying to envisage the scene... Geraldine Scott in the Danieli – how had she known where he was staying? had he told her? And why had she come so soon after having left him? It could have been no more than minutes since she'd disappeared with her daughter and bab-sia. Had she circled round through the inner streets behind the cathedral? past, say, San Zaccaria and onto the Riva? The packet was wrapped in shop paper; had he known Venice well he might have recognized the address. He could look it up later, go there and ask – perhaps that would provide some explanation. But what it would not provide nor shed light on was what may have gone through Carine's mind in the lobby when, most probably on her way out to meet him, she had heard this rather wild other woman speaking his name.

In the Molo he hesitated, dazed – he needed lunch. For an instant he stood equidistant between the pillars of the Lion and San Marco. Historical sense abating, he could not recall – he did not even wonder – whether this had been the spot for corona-tions or executions. A flood of fear was washing over him: that Carine may have thought she was at last facing some fancy of his, perhaps even an established liaison – the thing she most feared, now that the coffin of their hopes for a child had had the last nail driven into it. He felt a wild, keen, extending sadness of heart: her sadness, his sadness for her and for him. This was followed by anger: anger at this error, if error it was – if fears were correct – of her having to confront misapprehension and her fear in the form of a woman he did not now or ever seriously 'want'. So… was that the reason he'd found her sipping champagne next to Edmund, making no visible effort to get to Florian's for their date? Was it why she had left no note in the box to say she'd be late and to go on without her? Should he turn back then? But she was involved; and, if what he feared she was thinking were true, the awkwardness on both sides, and humiliation, was not to be exposed. Yet… shouldn't he go back and leave her a note? But what could it say? That 'nothing had happened'? Even though nothing had, or would or would even be thought of on his side, it hardly seemed enough – not, at any rate, for what she might have been thinking. Better to leave nothing – to amble off as if he too had been busy; as if he too were too tied up to fret over a tryst which, after all, was essentially frivolous, wasn't it? They slept with one another every night, didn't they? They saw one another every day, to such an extent as to make any but the most extreme dotard bored. Possibly too she had suspected nothing, not being the suspicious type – never had been. That was part of the reason she'd been a good wife; that theirs had been a marriage which had weathered the storm, despite the recurrent elf. (And where was *she* now? still wholly vanished? sucked away through the wild eye of Curt Burnham III? eclipsed in the rise of guilt with the advent of Geraldine Scott?) But wasn't that also part of what made his spirits sag and the 'inward romantic principle' take over, with its dissatisfied longings? How many nights had he waited for her to come home, standing at the window staring down on the garden, rapt for the sound of a cab? On occasion hadn't he even thought to call the police, growing full of some terrible vision of her rushing into the street, hand raised to hail taxi, being knocked down by some BMW careening drunkenly from the City to speed some hooligan home to his middle-class doxie in Fulham? At last she would arrive – eleven-thirty, quarter-to-one. 'Where have you been? I've been so worried!' What he could not have said then, of course – never had – was: 'I've been bored; I feel trapped; what is the point of long evenings in front of the TV, this long day's journey into old age with no prospect of children or even resurgence of passion?' But he couldn't; wouldn't. He loved her and would excuse her excuses ever, threadbare though on occasion they'd seemed. But he had remained angry, or at least frustrated. He loved her of course; but he was a man, and somewhere beneath this idea of a marriage – of faithfulness, of 'being good' – a slower and sadder demise was lurking: a soft, quiet bed and smell of cooked vegetables hanging in unventilated drapery.

Guilt increased. He banished thoughts, turning.

Santa Maria della Salute rose, calm, maternal, across the mouth of the canal. He started to walk. He would go over there, to the other side: it somehow beckoned, looking cooler and brighter at the same time, less trafficked, like a kind of blessed isle beyond this welter of funny hats, clicking cameras, dinosaur tails of collected gondolas. Down the front he passed, till he came to the traghetto a few steps beyond Harry's Bar. Harry's Bar – should he look in? He stepped over, opened the door, glimpsed the shipboard décor beyond entry partition... Americans on banquettes, once his own kind, in their Hemingway fantasy Europe. Why did they come here only to drink in Deco lounges beneath frosted glass, he wondered, recoiling. Venice outside could have been San Francisco for them, or some burg on Long Island. He retreated into the sweaty noon, though not before – or was it just as the sun restruck his eye? – he seemed to glimpse two familiars: Curt Burnham restored, no longer stroke-ridden, grinning conspiratorially in a booth at the back with the blonde who had buzzed Bahadin.

Could this be? If so, what did it signify? He felt impelled across the alley that debouched on the front. Did he see hurrying towards him, or maybe into Harry's door, the two gunsels in darkglasses – Bahadin's designer boys on their way to make a hit? Ach, this hallucinogenic consciousness!

Leaping onto the traghetto, he asked for a gondola, stepped in and was off. Slipping over the wavelets, he heard no gunshot nor crash of thugs into Harry's, nor confrontation with Burnham-as-CIA-operative mugging with a hit-woman to knock off a middle-Eastern arms-dealer. That was a film fantasy: an unreal world, not his Europe, not anyone's real life – though, of course, what was? The gondola rose up and slapped down, crossing the wake of a vaporetto. From the right gazed grand hotels: the Bauer-Grünwald, Gritti – ancient, storied palaces now given over to trade; the ubiquitous, all-sovereign tourist. Moving on out of sight beyond the Accademmia bridge stood Ca Foscari, Palazzo Mocenigo, haunts of Byron and heroes swirling back into the gloom of deepest Venetian legend. Geraldine appeared again in his mind – her gypsy shawl, her strange depths – to pass on, as the gondola with scant ease nudged its way between wooden posts and, paying, Tony stepped off to emerge into the shadow of the Dogana.

Straightening his jacket, suddenly as if breathing free, he strolled past mother church into a narrower, quieter passage. It soon led, as a sign said, towards the Guggenheim. Should he go there? But did he really want to wile away his time – for it was *his* now, he realized, Carine having left him to do as he pleased – in a courtyard redolent of a sort of grace to be found in West L.A.? Maybe, he thought, as he turned the corner of a thin, silent street. But then, by the entry, as if in reflection of his two minds, he came upon a young man of perhaps twenty and young woman of the same age. They had been strolling ahead: two benign, pretty forms with cropped heads, practical for summer, dressed in the haphazard, colourful rags that youth of all strata had always seemed to wear in vagabond Europe on hot holidays. They were German or Danish or Polish or Swede – it hardly mattered. What struck Tony like a force of destiny as he eyed them was the way the young man turned to her just by the Museum gate and, as if to ascertain whether to go in or not, slipped a hand up the loose shirt over her loose jeans and ever-so-slightly rubbed her tummy.

This sensual gesture – so natural, innocent, as if semiconscious – might have been remarkable in itself. But what made it so arresting in his psyche was that, as she turned, gentle-featured, with skin like a ripening peach, he could see for the first time that she was vastly pregnant: that the belly the boy stroked (they seemed almost too young to be parents) was not only a part of a young woman he loved but also the cocoon of his soon-to-be-born child.

The sight was so touching, so profoundly breath-stealing, that it held him like grace. Ending almost before it had begun, it vanished – they vanished; in or away, you could hardly tell. Yet the image remained; stuck there in his mind, indelible as some mystic's vision of God.

It held him as if with the soft touch of a hand; of young, clean fingertips on the heavenly, distended round of her skin, not quite seen but so lovingly felt, under the hang of a fading turquoise blouse…

Ah, he loved it. This was love, whatever the truth of their lives, or of any life. He absorbed it, the grace of the picture; drank it in, a grace that transcended desire to see other pictures, as in fond meditation he continued on his way through the afternoon streets.

Cling to this, his soul said. Cling to this gentle image! And it clung to him, blessing, protective, holding off for a time the indeterminate day.

The feeling continued, becoming diffuse, less specific, travelling down his body like some mild, calming drug. He went on, his steps softened, as if falling on moss instead of paving-stones by a canal – one of the little traverse waterways that led from the city-side towards the broader Canale della Guidecca and thence to real sea. Small three-storied buildings looked over the waters; small motor-launches bobbed at moorings. A line of laundry hung against a salmon-hued wall; a denizen of some cool inner place gazed out, leaning over a black, sculpted railing.

White plastic chairs sat around pink-clothed tables in front of a small hotel that he passed half-somnambulistically, having mislaid his hunger, lost in the beatitude. Here I might come for winter, he imagined; I'll find a room and just stay, live and drift, for so long as beatitude lasts. And why not? he thought on – though perhaps 'thought' is not exactly the word – as he came out, onto the Zattare allo Spirito Santo.

Sun blazed down very hot now, but it hardly phased him. To the northwest he made out more albergos, a pensione, more chairs by the canal, umbrella-tops flapping in light gusts of breeze. Should I sit? It was lovely, the sweep of sky and water and yet more Venice, a last of Venice, on the Guidecca across. But he kept on. A new church, flat-fronted, unmaternal; then another, somewhat smaller, to the far side... he looked in; stepped in – the arrangement austere, not baroque as expected, like some church in the City of London except for its ceiling. Gazing down out of it, flat and inlaid in squares of wood, were innumerable faces – of the saints, he supposed. Yes, he thought, resting, his neck arched and head back: this must be the Gesuati or some other Jesuit chapel; here are the mystics and wild visionaries, the odd madmen and women who fasted and wept, holding themselves from life, hiding in caves or in deserts, self-flagellating, dwelling among animals, doing whatever to raise sights to espy the transcendent, everlasting, glorious – *what*? Was it God? What was God, he wondered, slipping out of the church and carrying on, now less beatified, again carnal enough to worry about food...

The question too great. He took a chair in front of the next café, whose umbrellas advertised Coca-Cola and little blackboard offered pizza, wine and coffee for a popular price. It was somehow offensive, the question – he had thought so for years – like the price of hotels such as the Danieli. It was one thing to feel indeterminate grace or admire the beauty of a day or church ceiling, but to believe in 'God', even to dare to speak of that Unknowable, seemed an offence to intelligence, and taste. Maybe 'God' was there, but what did he know? What could anyone know – though here, in Italy, in Venice, it did seem quite natural, like sexual longing, or appetite or love for beauty, to incorporate some shade of religiosity into the whole...

Such ideas, too big. And here came the waiter, and went. And Tony rested, waiting for his food.

By his knife lay a packet – the book he had carried, forgotten, set down. He picked it up again, untaped the paper and slipped out *The Counterlife in Venice*, by Geraldine Scott. Red cover with medallions of faces – Byron, Browning, Pound – also facades of the famous palazzi, the one Wagner had died in for instance. How sweet of her to have left it, and so soon. Was there an inscription? yes, but only her name, with love. No address or card of hotel in the wrapper? not even the bookshop's receipt. How could he tell her what he thought once he'd read it, he wondered in the way a kind reader does when opening to the first page of a work by an author he knows:

'In this world of frenzy, sadness, error and war...'

Not a bad beginning. But he let the cover shut – won't read now; can't, he realized letting his eyes rest on the calm of the waters, the line of diminishing land and slightly-fleeced sky in a middle distance. And here came a slow tanker, marine blue, slightly rusting, its name, *Dalmatia,* in white visible from where he sat. Was it one of Bahadin's? The thought rose with brief visions of a Lebanon he had never seen, then closer to home the rolling hills around Mostar and Kosovo: a landscape too familiar in Europe from years of evening news.

'In this world of frenzy, sadness, error and war...' – promising first line indeed.

The elf passed, on the arm of Curt Burnham. The pair metamorphosed into a young couple in loose clothes in front of the Guggenheim gate. The pregnant girl faded into a vision from deeper memory – somewhere in northern California or an imagined landscape full of light: a young mother, bright-haired, wearing a shift or loose frock, planting seeds in her garden with an afternoon's sun behind silhouetting her form, while in the foreground on a middle-class lawn a little russet-haired child (it looked like a girl) sang contentedly under her breath as she pedalled in circles on a tricycle. This changed and the image became Carine, ebony curls haphazard, a smile on her lips, on the day when they had bought their first London flat. In a sleeveless red dress, bare-armed and barefoot, she whirled her skirts across the summer gardens outside – a whirl of inspiration half-suggesting a dance, which never quite came. Yet on that day at the least – Tony knew: he remembered – they had been completely happy.

***

– Venice, Berlin, 1998